s there anything else I need to bring?" Hayley asked as Luke walked with her to he door. "Besides the usual employment nformation, that is."

Not that I can think of."

Reaching for the doorknob, she studied him. He did ook more at ease than he had when she'd arrived.

She opened the door and stepped outside, glad the nterview was over and that they'd agreed on the details. "I'll see you and Brayden in the morning, hen," she said, turning back to look at him. "And hank you."

My pleasure," he said.

For the first time, she saw his smile. It nearly blew her away. Without the frown and rigid exterior or the distracted and desperate actions, he was gorgeous. And she was going to be working for him.

Not good. Not good at all.

Dear Reader,

Being a parent is one of the most difficult jobs a person can undertake. Parenting requires on-the-job training as a caregiver, doctor, teacher, spiritual adviser, friend and mortal enemy (according to an angry child). The nights are late and the mornings are early. A good day can turn bad in an instant. A bad day can turn good with a hug or a simple smile. There are tears and giggles, joy and heartache. Parenting is often made easier with two parents, but that isn't always the way life happens.

According to the U.S. Census Bureau, there are approximately 13.6 million single parents in the United States, responsible for raising 21.2 million children or roughly 26% of children under 21. Those numbers don't include only single moms. Single-father homes have grown almost 60% in the past ten years.

Child care for children of single-parent families can be difficult to find, but Luke Walker's sister has sent him a young woman to be the nanny for his small son. One look at the woman has him convinced that she's not the person for them. But like parenting, love can happen with a hug or a simple smile.

Welcome back to Desperation, Oklahoma, where hearts meet at the most unexpected times.

Best wishes and happy reading!

Roxann

A Nanny for the Cowboy

ROXANN DELANEY

HARLEQUIN® AMERICAN ROMANCE®

Recycling programs
for this product may
not exist in your area.

ISBN-13: 978-0-373-75448-9

A NANNY FOR THE COWBOY

This edition published by arrangement with Harlequin Books S.A.

For questions and comments about the quality of this book, please contact us at CustomerService@Harlequin.com.

Printed in U.S.A.

ABOUT THE AUTHOR

Roxann Delaney doesn't remember a time when she wasn't reading or writing, and she always loved that touch of romance in both. A native Kansan, she's lived on a farm, in a small town and has returned to live in the city where she was born. Her four daughters and grandchildren keep her busy when she isn't writing or designing websites. The 1999 Maggie Award winner is excited to be a part of the Harlequin American Romance line and loves to hear from readers. Contact her at roxann@roxanndelaney.com or visit her website, www.roxanndelaney.com.

Books by Roxann Delaney

HARLEQUIN AMERICAN ROMANCE

1194—FAMILY BY DESIGN
1269—THE RODEO RIDER
1292—BACHELOR COWBOY
1313—THE LAWMAN'S LITTLE SURPRISE
1327—THE RELUCTANT WRANGLER
1357—THE MAVERICK'S REWARD

Pat, Theresa, Deborah, Kathie and Kristi,
I'd be lost without you all.

Love and hugs.

Chapter One

Luke Walker peeled back the edge of the curtain to get a glimpse of the woman getting out of her car in his driveway. "Not on your life, lady," he muttered.

Ignoring the tug on the leg of his jeans, he watched what should have been a prospective employee walk up the path leading to the house. But *walk* was the wrong thing to call the seductive advance. Panthers on the prowl were less graceful.

The wind caught the young woman's long, straight dark hair, blowing it over one shoulder, and she reached up to brush it back with her fingers. Luke saw very little of any of it, focused instead on her long legs in the trim, short skirt she wore.

He must've been crazy to let his sister talk him into interviewing the woman. He'd always thought his sister had more sense than to send him someone who looked remotely like a Miss America contestant. But if he really thought about it, Erin had done some far from smart things in her life.

The doorbell rang, dragging a moan from deep within his chest. How would he manage to send this woman away without hurting her feelings? Erin would skin him alive if she learned he hadn't hired the vixen waiting at the door. And if he hurt the woman's feelings in the process, he'd never hear the end of it. Even worse, if he didn't hire her, who would he find to—

"Up! Wannup!"

"Not now, Brayden. Be good and let go." Reaching down, he pried the two-year-old's chubby arms from his legs and noticed the smear of grape jelly Brayden left in his wake. Taking the toddler by one of his gooey hands, Luke moved to the front door as the bell chimed a second time. "Be there in a sec!" he called.

There wasn't time to wipe Brayden's hands. Not with the woman ringing the damn bell every two seconds. Where the hell had Brayden gotten the jelly, anyway? But Luke wasn't eager to check out the source, even if he had the time. Which he didn't. No telling what kind of damage the kitchen was in, after a visit from Brayden.

Drawing in a deep breath, Luke reached for the doorknob, hoping he could make the interview as brief and as painless as possible—for both of them. But when he opened the door, his son wrapped both arms around his legs again in the two-year-old equivalent of a vise-like grip, throwing Luke completely off balance. He managed to save himself from falling by bracing his hand against the door frame.

"Mr. Walker?" the young woman asked, slipping off a pair of dark glasses he hadn't even noticed.

"Uh, yeah, that's me." Distracted by the need to keep his balance, Luke tried to concentrate on presenting a formidable appearance. Not an easy feat, he decided, with a jelly-smeared son attached at his knees, and made even worse by the deep blue of the woman's eyes.

Her gaze traveled down to where Brayden held Luke in a death grip and moved back up again. She smiled and extended her hand. "I'm Hayley. Hayley Brooks? Your sister—"

"Yeah. Erin. My sister." He cringed and hoped she didn't notice, as he took her hand and gave it the briefest of shakes, then immediately let go. He wasn't quick enough. A wave of warmth snaked quickly up his arm. This was not a good thing.

"I guess this is Brayden." She knelt to the little boy's level. "Hi, Brayden."

Brayden hid his face behind Luke's legs and shook his head. Luke reached down and ruffled his son's curly hair. "He's a little shy."

Straightening, she faced him. "Typical two-year-old," she said with a blazing smile. "Now, about the job…"

"The job," Luke echoed. He didn't have a clue what to say to this woman. He desperately needed someone to take care of his son, but this one wasn't the type of someone he'd had in mind. Nope, not even close.

Before he had a chance to make up an excuse that wouldn't hurt her feelings, Brayden let out an earsplitting wail. The grip on Luke's legs tightened, but he finally managed to extricate himself and hauled the boy into his arms, jelly and all. "Maybe this isn't such a good time," he told the prospective nanny, over the howls coming from his son.

"It's as good a time as any." She reached out and took Brayden in her arms, completely oblivious to the goo.

Brayden immediately quieted.

Luke stared at the pair.

"There," she said, brushing the front of Brayden's hair away from his forehead with her fingers. "Isn't that better?" Turning to Luke, who was struck speechless, she smiled. "If I can just come inside?"

"Oh. Yeah, sure," Luke answered, completely taken off guard. He stepped back, waiting until she'd moved through the doorway and past him with his silent but somber son in her arms. "It's kind of a mess," he warned, more than aware of the state of the house.

"It usually is with little ones around." She flashed him yet another smile and followed him into the living room. Moving aside the newspaper he'd earlier unfolded while he waited for her, she took a seat on the sofa and settled Brayden on her lap. "There are five kids in my family. My mom says she doesn't know what to do with a neat house, now that we're grown."

Luke barely heard her. He was watching his son, whose attention was on the brightly painted wooden beads of the woman's necklace, nestled in the V-neck of her top. When Brayden reached for the beads with his chubby hands, Luke tensed, prepared to grab the child before more damage could be done other than sharing the jelly. Holding his breath, he wondered how he could intercept the disaster he knew was coming, without frightening the woman.

"Would you mind sitting?" he heard her say.

He jerked his gaze away from the beads at her throat to stare at her. "What?"

"I'm sorry," she answered with an apologetic smile. "It's awkward having to look up at you. Would you mind sitting?"

Without replying, he continued to keep his attention on his son, while he tentatively perched on the chair facing the sofa, ready to intervene when needed. He loved his son to distraction, but he also knew firsthand that Brayden could leave disaster in his wake in the blink of an eye. And those beads were obviously intriguing the little guy.

She shifted Brayden in her lap, but completely ignored the boy's hand on her necklace. "What time does your day start, Mr. Walker?"

"Early," he answered. "I get up around five and am out of the house by seven." Or at least he tried to be. With Brayden to get out of bed, dressed and fed, it was more often later. Much later.

"Who watches Brayden that early?"

Luke looked down at his work-worn hands. "Right now, nobody." He glanced up at her and hurried to add, "I mean, I've been taking him with me later in the morning, when I can't find someone to watch him."

"Have you checked into day care in town?"

He nodded, thinking of the hassle it had been for everyone. "We tried it, but the best place was full before it even opened. And it isn't like my hours are nine to five or anything. There are some days that I don't need to leave the house until later, and I can't see taking Brayden to town when he doesn't need to be there."

"I see."

Luke wasn't sure he liked the way she said that. The real problem was that both he and Brayden had taken an instant dislike to the woman at the day care center that did have an empty slot. Several, in fact. They were on the list at Libby Miles's new place, but had been warned the wait might be a long one.

"Let me put it this way," he said, uncomfortable about sharing everything. "They charged me the same, no matter what time I took him in or what time I picked him up, or even whether he was there at all. That's a waste."

"I understand how difficult it can be," she answered, as Brayden scrambled down from her lap. "I grew up on a farm, so I know what work schedules can be like. I think we can find an arrangement that works for both of us."

Luke's first reaction was to breathe a sigh of relief, until he realized that he'd already decided not to hire the woman. Having met his sister's candidate, he suspected Erin was doing a little matchmaking, and he wasn't about to let that happen. If he was smart, he wouldn't let this go any further. "I'm sure we could, but—"

Frowning, he pulled the ringing cell phone from his pocket and saw the caller was his brother. "I need to get this," he said, in lieu of an apology for the interruption. Standing, he made sure Brayden was busy playing with his toys, before crossing the room and hitting the talk button.

Just when I was getting up the nerve to send her on her way.

"Yeah?" he barked into the phone.

"I'm glad I caught you," Dylan said. "I need to tell you something."

Luke turned his back to the woman and kept his

voice low. "Make it quick, will ya? I'm interviewing that niece of Erin's friend."

"Interviewing? Oh, yeah," Dylan replied. "To take care of Brayden. Hope that's going good."

"Not really." Luke sneaked a quick look at the nanny he couldn't hire over his shoulder and saw that her attention was on his son. "But that's my problem," he told his brother. "So what do you need to tell me?"

There was silence for a moment until Dylan finally spoke. "I'm taking off for a couple of weeks."

"Taking off?" Luke asked. "Again?"

Dylan's heavy sigh echoed across the wires. "I gotta get away, Luke. I can't explain it. I just gotta get away."

"To where?"

"I don't know yet. Maybe I'll go down and visit Erin. Or maybe I won't. I just know I need some time away from the ranch. From everything."

Luke's first thought was to tell his brother that he couldn't leave right now. Not until arrangements were made for Brayden's day care. For years, Luke had tried to talk to Dylan about his annual disappearance, but because Luke suspected those weeks had to do with the anniversary of their parents' death, he hadn't pushed it. Getting away always seemed to help Dylan, so maybe it would be a good idea to keep quiet.

"Okay," Luke finally answered. "If that's what you need. When are you leaving?"

"As soon as I finish loading up my truck."

"That soon?" Luke tried to conceal his surprise. "When will you be back?"

"A week. Maybe two. It depends."

Luke did a quick mental check of what would need

to be done during his brother's absence. "I can cover it," he promised.

They ended the conversation and, as he slowly put his phone back in his pocket, Luke realized there was only one way he could make good on his promise. Without Dylan around, he'd have to have someone to care for Brayden. There was no way around it.

He shook his head. He'd let his brother put him somewhere between a rock and a hard place, and it was damned uncomfortable.

HAYLEY TRIED HER BEST to ignore the one-sided phone conversation going on across the room and concentrated on getting to know the little boy playing on the floor beside her.

Getting down to his level, she knelt next to him and watched him gather the small plastic cows. "Do you help your daddy with chores, Brayden?"

His hands stilled and he looked up at her. "Cows."

She picked one of the animals from the pile and held it up. "Yes, a cow. Do you have cows?"

He continued to stare at her for a moment and then returned to his play.

"Miss Brooks?"

Hayley looked up to see Luke Walker towering over her. "I was just getting to know Brayden," she explained. Taking the hand he offered to help her stand, she wished she hadn't. Unlike when they'd met at the door, only minutes before, this time she felt the male strength it held—along with a totally unwanted flash of…something. She'd make sure not to let it happen again.

He released her, raking his other hand through his light brown hair. She recognized the sign of distress and noticed that his eyes mirrored it. "The phone call was bad news?"

"No. Yes." He shook his head. "A minor setback is all. Short-term."

She waited patiently for him to continue. She wasn't comfortable about being hired out of what she was fairly sure was desperation. It certainly didn't say much for her skills. But she did need the job, and she would be a fool not to accept the position.

When he didn't elaborate, she realized she would have to ask for the information she needed. "When would you like me to start?"

"Start?"

She nodded, wondering if Luke Walker was stable and if she wouldn't be better off looking for a job somewhere else. But she'd promised her Aunt Rita that she would do what she could for her friend's brother. She couldn't back out now.

"Start the job," she clarified, adding a smile she didn't particularly feel at the moment.

He lowered himself to the chair and shook his head, looking like a man who didn't have a clue what was going on. "As soon as possible, I guess," he answered.

Hayley tried her best to be patient. The interview wasn't going nearly as well as she'd hoped. "Possible for you or me?"

"For you, of course," he replied, as if she should know it.

"All right." She took her seat on the sofa again. "We've determined that your day begins early," she said, hoping to move things along. "That isn't a problem for me. I have some things to attend to later today, so if I arrive at, say, six-thirty tomorrow, will that work for you?"

"Six-thirty?"

"In the morning." It was clear that his mind wasn't on their conversation, and she started to rise. "If you would rather we discuss this at another time—"

"No!" he said, startling her. She regained her composure and waited while he ran his hand through his hair a second time. "Look, I'm sorry," he said, his distress evident in his deep blue eyes. "Please, don't leave. Please. It's just that I— Damn, this is a mess," he finished as a mutter.

Hayley let her guard down and her heart ached for him. She didn't know what, in particular, the problem was, but she had some sort of idea. From her aunt Rita, she'd learned that Luke Walker was a single dad, struggling to raise his young son after his wife had walked out on them a year and a half before, apparently without a backward glance. He and his brother ran this ranch near Desperation, Oklahoma, where they'd grown up and, according to her aunt, didn't lack for money, thanks to excellent business practices and several active oil wells the family owned. To Hayley, that meant she wouldn't have to worry about being paid. She quickly reminded herself that he hadn't actually made the offer yet, but she was determined to be positive about it.

"You know ranching, right?" he asked.

She nodded. "As I said, I grew up on a small farm,

although my brothers do most of the work, now that my dad has retired."

"Yeah, I know how that can be." His eyes darkened with sadness. "We've had our own struggles in the past."

"I understand that you and your brother operate the ranch," she said, hoping to draw him out enough to discover what was bothering him. If she was going to work for him, she needed to know if this problem would affect her employment—or his son—in any way.

"Yes, the two of us," he said, nodding. "This house is on the southern edge of the property. Dylan, my older brother, lives in the same house were we grew up, but north of here. I built this house when—" He stopped for a moment, seemingly lost in thought, then squared his shoulders. "A few years ago." Leaning forward, he caught her gaze and held it. "If you can start tomorrow, I'd really appreciate it. Dylan will be gone for a week or two, meaning I'll have more chores to do. That means I'll have less time to watch after Brayden." He looked at his son, quietly playing with his toys, and then back at her. "He seems to like you, which is something, considering he's never had much to do with anybody since— Well, for a long time."

She guessed that the "long time" he mentioned must have been since Brayden's mother left. "I can be here at six-thirty or whenever is best tomorrow," she said. "But you need to know that I have classes on Monday, Wednesday and Friday evenings, and will have to leave here by six."

"That's not a problem," he said, getting to his feet

and walking toward her. "I guess you already know what the salary is?"

"Yes," she answered. "Your sister sent the details in a letter." Gathering her things, she stood and offered her hand. "Then I'll see you in the morning, Mr. Walker."

He hesitated before taking it. When he did, the contact made her warm all over, and she couldn't seem to pull away. His eyes held a surprised but quizzical gleam, and she wasn't sure what to think of it or of her own reaction.

"Wouldn't a first name basis be better?" he asked.

His voice seemed lower and his gaze held her. Gently removing her hand from his, she tried for a smile. "Yes, it—it probably would be. *Luke*."

"Good," he said, in a more businesslike manner, while taking a step back. "I'll see you in the morning."

Convinced she'd imagined things, she turned to his son and took a fortifying breath before saying goodbye. "I'll see you tomorrow, Brayden, okay? And I'll bring a special treat." She turned to his dad. "If that's all right."

"Sure. No problem."

"Is there anything else I need to bring?" she asked, as he walked with her to the door. "Besides the usual employment information, that is."

"Not that I can think of."

Reaching for the doorknob, she studied him. He still didn't appear to be aware of everything, but he did look more at ease than he had when she'd arrived.

She opened the door and stepped outside, glad the interview was over and that they'd agreed on the details. "I'll see you and Brayden in the morning then," she said, turning back to look at him. "And thank you."

"My pleasure," he said.

For the first time, she saw his smile. It nearly blew her away. Without the frown and rigid exterior or the definitely distracted and desperate actions, he was gorgeous. And *she* was going to be working for him. Not good. Not good at all.

LUKE SURVEYED THE LAST of the rooms and looked at his watch. Brayden's new nanny would be arriving at any minute. He'd worked his butt off, trying to get the house as clean and tidy as possible in the short time he'd had. But there'd been other things to deal with, too. Dylan had stopped by with a list of chores, as if Luke had never done the job before, and had been in bad shape. It was easy to see that a vacation from the ranch was needed, and Luke didn't mind taking care of things near as much as he had when Dylan had first given him the news.

Luke was picking up one of Brayden's toys from behind a chair when he heard a car pull into the drive. "Keep it professional, man," he muttered to himself on his way to open the door. "She's your employee."

But as soon as he opened the door and saw her standing there in a tight pair of blue jeans and shirt that definitely failed to hide her curves, he knew he was in trouble.

"Good morning," she said, stepping past him and into the house.

Closing the door behind her, he followed her, keeping his attention on the cardboard box she held in her arms, instead of the view of her enticing backside. "What's in the box?"

"The special treat I mentioned."

He hadn't expected anything quite so large. "That's a pretty big special treat."

She looked over her shoulder at him on her way into the living room and gave him a sheepish grin. "Synchronicity."

"What?"

Setting the box on a small table, she opened it and peered inside. "Synchronicity. An unexpected but happy coincidence." She pulled out an old metal replica of a farm truck with a small plastic cow and calf in the back. "My mom was getting ready to throw these out a few days ago," she explained, turning to look at him. "Apparently, my brothers didn't want them, so I said I'd take them. I didn't know why, but I see now that it was because of Brayden. I hope he'll enjoy them. I remember how much we did."

Luke took the truck from her and studied it. "I think I had one like this. Can't buy them like this anymore."

"Exactly," she said. "I noticed how much Brayden enjoys his farm toys, so I thought, why not? It's okay, isn't it? I mean, you don't mind, do you?"

He looked up at the sound of hesitancy in her voice and wished he hadn't. Damn those blue eyes! "Yes," he managed to answer.

"Oh." She ducked her head and took the truck from him, returning it to the box. "I'm sorry, I didn't realize..."

"I meant that it was okay," he hurried to assure her. "I don't mind. Brayden will get a kick out of it." He pulled out a small tractor and set it on the table, then peered into the box. "What else is in there?"

She shrugged. “Some wooden building blocks and more farm toys.”

Luke reached into the box at the same time she did, accidentally brushing her hand, and immediately jerked away. Just touching her rattled him, but he pulled himself together before he spoke. “Brayden’s still asleep, but I know he’ll like everything. So… Maybe I should show you around before I have to get to work.”

She returned the toys to the box and closed it. Squaring her shoulders, she stepped away. “Yes, that’s a good idea, although I’m sure I’ll know my way around in no time at all.”

He didn’t doubt she would. She was that kind of woman. Or at least he suspected she was. But it didn’t really matter, he thought, as he led her from the living room, through the dining room and into the kitchen. Once she settled into her job of taking care of Brayden, he wouldn’t be spending that much time around her. A quick hello in the morning and a goodbye before she left in the evening, and that would be it.

“Nice kitchen,” she said.

Her voice pulled him out of his reverie. “Thanks. Let me know if we’re out of anything.” He thought about the nearly bare cabinets and refrigerator, and added, “I’ll make a trip into town for groceries later. There’s plenty of meat in the extra freezer, out in the garage, but Brayden likes peanut butter and jelly.”

“I noticed,” she said with a throaty chuckle.

He wasn’t sure whether to be embarrassed or laugh with her. “Yeah, I figured you did,” he said, giving in to the latter and adding his own chuckle. From the kitchen area, he walked to the attached family room and pointed to the corner, crowded with toys. "Brayden usually plays in here. We both spend more time in here than anywhere else. Except maybe outside."

She looked around, as if assessing the place. "Having the kitchen close by while he plays makes it handy."

He wasn't about to admit that they didn't spend all that much time in the kitchen, so he checked his watch and realized that he needed to get busy. "I'll show you the upstairs, before I go."

"Is that where Brayden's room is?" When he nodded, she turned back, obviously headed for the living room. "You go on, then," she said, over her shoulder. "I can find my way. I'll just put the toys I brought with his others and then check on him."

Luke felt like he was being a lousy employer, if he couldn't even spare the time to properly show her around. "Well, I—"

"No, it's all right. Really. I've probably made you late."

He stood in the doorway staring at her, stunned by her self-assurance. She reminded him of his sister, but she wasn't nearly as bossy as Erin. This woman didn't seem to let anything daunt her, and he begrudgingly admired her for it.

Great. One more thing to admire her for, when he was having enough trouble keeping his attention away from those long legs and those blue eyes and those—

"Will you be wanting dinner at noon?"

Luke quickly dragged his thoughts from where they shouldn't be and shook his head. "I'll just come in and grab a quick sandwich or something. Too much work to stop for anything, with Dylan gone."

But instead of hurrying off to start his workday, he settled on the arm of the sofa and watched her neaten the room he'd spent a good hour straightening before she arrived. He didn't mind, though. He liked the fact that she was tidy, and he'd make sure he didn't cause her any more work than was necessary.

With a throw pillow cradled to her chest, she turned to face him. "This is a very nice house. Comfortable and…nice. Brayden's mother must have very good taste."

Luke stiffened. He'd been working on not letting the past bother him so much and wished he'd found a way to avoid what needed to be said. Besides, if she was going to be his son's nanny, she deserved to know at least some of what had happened.

"Kendra left," he answered, the words as stiff as his body. "Almost a year and a half ago. And hasn't been back since."

"With no explanation?"

"None." But he knew that was a lie. There'd been Kendra's form of an explanation—a tantrum in the middle of the night. One of many that had come on not long after Brayden's birth. But he didn't think Brayden's nanny needed to know about that.

"She hasn't contacted him? A phone call? Note?"

Ready to put an end to the subject, Luke got to his feet. "Nothing. And I don't expect she ever will." He fervently hoped she never would. Brayden was his now. Kendra had even signed the papers, giving him full and complete custody, and relinquishing all parental rights.

"I'm sorry," she said, standing. "That's sad. For all of you."

He didn't agree at all, but he didn't say so. He didn't miss his ex-wife at all, and Brayden didn't remember her. They did fine without her or anyone. One mistake was enough, and he didn't have plans to repeat it.

He walked on to the door, and she followed. When he opened it and stepped out onto the porch, he noticed the suitcases on the ground by her car. "What are those?" he asked, turning back to find her standing in the doorway.

"My things."

He looked again at the suitcases and then at her, totally confused. "What kind of things?"

Her expression was one of complete surprise. "Why, my clothes and…and other things."

Nothing was making sense to him. "Why?"

She was now standing in front of him, plainly as confused as he was. "Because I can't wear the same thing every day, now can I?"

Every day? Why would she need— When it hit him, he couldn't believe he'd been so distracted by everything going on that he hadn't made himself clear. "You thought the job was for a live-in nanny?"

Her face paled and she took an unsteady step back, one hand going to her throat as her eyes widened. "It isn't?"

Chapter Two

Hayley was afraid her legs weren't going to hold her, but somehow she managed to continue standing. Her face began to burn with the heat of embarrassment, while she tried to make sense of what had gone wrong. She'd assumed her position would be that of a live-in nanny. Apparently that's not what Luke had in mind. Why hadn't they discussed it the day before, during the interview? There was no excuse, except that he'd been distracted, and she'd needed the job to help pay for her college tuition.

Glancing at her new employer, she realized he looked as if he'd been punched, and she wished she could think of something to say that would make everything all right. Absolutely nothing came to mind.

He glanced at his watch, then over his shoulder before turning his attention to her. "I know this is something we need to get settled, but—" He looked down, shaking his head. "It's not like it isn't important, because it is, but I need to get the chores done."

In the distance, she could hear the bellowing of cattle, obviously waiting to be fed. She wasn't sure if it was a good idea to let him walk away without settling the question of her employment, but she knew the importance of feeding livestock on time. "It's all right," she told him, hoping he didn't pick up on her insecurity. "We can settle it later."

He visibly relaxed, although his smile was shaky, at best. "Great. I mean, thanks. We'll do it at lunch." He started to move away, but stopped. "If that's okay." When she nodded, he let out a long breath. "Then I'll be back around noon."

Seeing that things were as settled as they could be for the time being, she turned for the house. She was nearly inside when she heard him call to her.

"I'll just put these suitcases on the porch, until we decide what we're going to do."

"That's fine. I'll just..." What? Worry? She couldn't say that, and she needed to reassure him that all would be well, even if *she* wasn't all that sure they would be. "I'll check on Brayden and get his breakfast started."

She didn't wait for an answer and, once inside with the door closed firmly behind her, she did her best to put aside the fear and disappointment that she might not have a job after all. Knowing that staying busy would help keep her from thinking of her current dilemma, she went upstairs and found Brayden's room. She soon had him awake and out of bed, so they could start their day. He didn't make a sound as she dressed him or while he ate his breakfast. When he finished eating, she checked the kitchen cabinets and pantry with thoughts of lunch and supper in mind, while he played in the family room with the toys she'd brought for him.

"Cow!" he announced, holding the plastic animal up for her to see.

"And a lovely cow it is," she said, laughing. She

hoped it wasn't the only word he knew. After all, he was two and should have a better vocabulary than one word.

Later, when Brayden began to rub his eyes, Hayley took him upstairs to his bed for a nap before lunch, then she returned to the kitchen. She expected Luke to appear at any time, and she'd planned to have a more substantial meal ready for him and Brayden. But between her disgust at herself for assuming things she shouldn't and the fact that there was practically nothing to eat in the house, she was left with literally throwing together some sandwiches.

"How's it going?"

She turned to see the object of her thoughts standing in the doorway, and she searched for something to say. "I wasn't sure if you like mayonnaise, but since I couldn't find any—" She pressed her lips together, realizing she was complaining, and went back to the preparations. It took every bit of her concentration to place the thick slices of ham, tomatoes and cheese between the pieces of bread. There was no reason to let him know how nervous he made her, and she quickly chalked it up to her fear of losing the job. No matter whether it was live-in or not, she needed it to help pay off her student loan and finish her master's degree. Not only that, but after a few hours with Brayden, she'd already fallen for the little boy.

Determined not to worry, she stacked the sandwiches on a plate. When she turned around, she was surprised to see Luke across the island counter from her.

"You didn't need to do this," he said as she placed the plate in front of him.

"It's all right," she answered with a shrug. "I consider it to be part of the job." If she still had a job.

He settled on a tall, upholstered stool and picked up a sandwich. "I appreciate it. Today's a little crazy, but it'll get better."

Instead of answering, she nodded and placed a glass of iced tea near his plate. "Lemon or sugar?"

"No, nothing. This is great."

They fell silent as he ate and she started a quick cleanup. The quiet, along with not knowing where she stood when it came to the job, nearly made her physically ill, and she decided it was time to ask if he'd made a decision. "Mr. Walker? I mean, Luke," she corrected immediately. He turned to look at her and she took a deep breath. "I just wanted to apologize—"

"Wait." He held up his hand. "I need to say something, but I'm not sure how to go about it. And I'm a little embarrassed. What I tried to say earlier was that it was my fault you'd gotten the wrong impression about the job, and I…well, *I* apologize."

The air whooshed out of her chest. Here she was, ready to apologize again, and he was taking the blame. She felt a small, warm glow of appreciation.

"Look, I know I shouldn't make excuses, but it's been a rough couple of years," he continued. "I should have been clear to you and my sister about what I expected in a nanny, instead of letting Erin handle things."

"Apology accepted." She smiled, hoping that he would see she was sincere. And she was, but they still needed to settle the live-in situation. "Have you—" She cleared her throat, determined to get it over with. "Have you made a decision about whether I'll be staying?"

He didn't speak for a moment. "I don't really need someone here all the time," he explained, "and I'd pay extra for your gas and time, if that's what's bothering you."

"It isn't that," she told him, although she had worried about the extra expense. "Driving back and forth leaves me very little time to study."

"Right. I forgot you mentioned school. What kind of classes are you taking?"

Because he seemed genuinely interested, she answered. "I'm working on my master's degree in hope of becoming a PA."

"PA?"

"Physician's assistant."

There was a spark of interest in his eyes. "That's like almost a doctor, right?"

She tried not to laugh. "Well, a little."

"I'm impressed. So how much longer until you have your degree?"

"In May. If I'm lucky." She didn't add that without the job, she'd have nowhere to live. She'd been sharing a small efficiency apartment in the city with another nurse, but her roommate had gotten married. She couldn't afford a place on her own. Not with college expenses to pay. The live-in nanny job was perfect for her, especially since she loved children.

"Then you'll be looking for a medical job?"

"That's the plan. Whether I find one or not is the question."

He fell silent for a moment. "I probably could use the extra help," he finally said, although there was a hesitancy in his voice. “And Brayden obviously took to you. Any problems this morning?”

She shook her head, thinking of the darling little boy who had wanted to share everything he could with her, from his toys to his view out the window overlooking the patio. “He was an angel. He even took a morning nap without prodding, and that’s not very common for someone his age. Two-year-olds will sometimes fight until they drop.”

Luke’s grin revealed his good humor. “It’s usually next thing to a world war when I try to put him down. You must have the knack. But I’ll warn you, it may not last.”

As if on cue, Brayden appeared in the doorway, his curly hair sticking out in every direction. “Wanna dink.”

Hayley hurried over to him and scooped him into her arms. “And how about a sandwich to go with that *dink?*” she asked him as she gave him a hug.

“Sammich!” He wiggled in her arms, but she managed to hold tight until she pulled the high chair over next to his dad and set him in it.

“He’s a bright little guy,” she told Luke. While father and son chattered at each other, she retrieved the jelly sandwich she’d prepared for Brayden earlier and poured a cup of milk.

“You managed to find your way around?” Luke asked.

“Yes,” she answered, tying a bib around Brayden’s neck. “It’s a beautiful house. And so much room, too,” she added, but suddenly wished she hadn’t.

He put his elbow on the table and propped his chin

in his hand, obviously comfortable with the question, unlike earlier. "You like it?"

She took a seat on the other side of Brayden, and answered without thinking. "Who wouldn't?"

Fearing it had been the wrong thing to say, she held her breath as Luke shrugged and pushed away from the counter. "It's just big," he said. "More room than Brayden and I need, that's for sure." He ruffled his son's hair and stood. "You need to leave by six, right?"

"No, not tonight. I have early classes on Monday, Wednesday and Friday."

"You'll need a little time to settle in, then. I can be done by six."

"If that works for you, I won't argue. Would it be all right if I take Brayden into town, after lunch?" she asked, then hurried to add, "I'll make sure he gets a longer nap when we get back. I'd like to pick up some groceries, if you don't mind, and Brayden might enjoy the outing."

Luke rubbed his chin with his knuckles and nodded. "Yeah, we do need some stuff." He gave her a sheepish smile. "I never seem to know what to get and usually end up with nothing I need and everything I don't."

She cleaned the jelly from Brayden's face and hands and helped him down from the chair. "Don't worry about it," she told Luke. "I'll get you back up to par with the food."

"I'll call the grocery store and have them charge it to me."

She nodded. "Just give me a limit, and I'll go from there."

"Whatever we need," he said with a shrug. "No limit."

She wasn't accustomed to buying food for someone she didn't know and hoped she would make wise decisions. Brayden was easy to figure out, but she wasn't so sure about his dad. "Is there anything special you like?" she asked.

"Just about everything. Meat and potatoes or whatever. I'm not picky, as long as it's easy to fix. No need for you to spend a lot of time cooking." He glanced at his watch and frowned. "I'd better get back to work, or I won't be done by six."

"I only need to know where Brayden's car seat is, and we'll be all set for the rest of the day."

He walked to the doorway that led to the garage, but didn't open the door. "The spare is out here. I hardly use it, so just keep it in your car. I can get it for you."

"No need," she said in a rush. "I'll find it. I've taken up enough of your time."

He gave a quick nod. When Brayden ran to him and clasped his arms around his daddy's legs, Luke reached down and mussed his hair. "I'll be back later, buddy. You be good for Hayley, okay?"

Both of them looked at Hayley, and she offered them a smile. "We'll be fine."

"Well, okay then," Luke said, while removing his son from his legs. "I'll bring your suitcases in. I guess you saw that there's a spare room right around the corner there."

"Yes, a very nice room. It'll be fine. Thank you."

"And you can put your car in the garage, too." he told her, and she thanked him again.

Hesitating, he finally opened the door and left without saying anything else. Hayley breathed a sigh of pure relief. She had a job. And she loved Brayden. But her new boss unnerved her. One minute he was all business and unwilling to talk, and she could handle that. But when he loosened up and became what she suspected was the real Luke Walker, she felt that old, familiar fluttery feeling in her stomach. That same feeling she'd had when she first met Nathan. But that had eventually turned sour, and she'd ended it, relieved that she did. She'd learned a lesson from the whole experience, and now she was determined to concentrate on finishing school. She'd simply focus on her studies and her tiny charge until that fluttering went away.

LUKE DRIED HIS HANDS on the towel and checked the time. *Right on the dot.* He wasn't late.

Opening the door leading from the garage mudroom to the house, he was nearly bowled over by the mouth-watering smells coming from the kitchen. He hadn't had the pleasure of enjoying a home-cooked meal for longer than he wanted to admit, but he sure hadn't forgotten what it was like.

He spied Hayley in the kitchen and looked around. To his surprise, he found Brayden playing quietly in the corner with the toys she'd brought him. For the past year and a half, his son had been like a burr, sticking to him at all times. He wasn't sure what magic Hayley was working or how she was doing it, but he was happy to see Brayden being more like a kid should be.

Hunkering down next to the boy, he pointed at the

plastic pony Brayden held. "Hey, guy, whatcha got there?"

Brayden looked up at him. "Sorsey," he answered and put the pony in his dad's hand.

Luke chuckled at Brayden's habit of replacing an *S* for an *H* in words. "Yep, it sure is. And a mighty fine one, too."

Spying a plastic cowboy, he picked it up and studied it. Remembering the similar set he and Dylan had played with when they were small boys, he felt the oddly familiar ache in his chest as memories of his own childhood flooded him. His early years had been happy and normal, but the later ones had brought sorrow, and he quickly pushed aside the painful thoughts.

"So how'd you and Hayley get along, Brayden? Everything go okay?"

His son looked up at him, his dark brown eyes round and full of an innocence Luke knew came and went with the wind. As if he suddenly understood, Brayden turned to look at the new nanny and responded with a throaty giggle, a sure sign that he and Hayley had hit it off.

Tugging at one of Brayden's short curls, Luke smiled and kept his voice low. "Yeah, that's what I figured. You got your old man's good taste in women."

When he realized what he had just said to his son, Luke clamped his mouth shut. *Good taste*? Hardly. He had been so sure that Kendra was the one-and-only girl for him. He'd been as wrong as anybody could ever be. If he could turn back the clock…

Beside him, Brayden bumped the truck against his knee. No, no turning back the clock. Kendra had given him the one thing he cared about more than life itself. Even the ranch didn't hold a candle to the way he felt about his son. And Brayden was all his.

Getting to his feet, Luke walked the length of the long room. "Something sure smells good," he said as he walked through the room to stand behind her. He breathed in, just as he remembered his manners. "But you really didn't have to go to so much trouble."

She glanced over her shoulder at him and moved to her left, away from him. "No trouble. I did some shopping today. It's in the slow cooker. It's ready, whenever you are."

"I sure appreciate it." She looked up and he caught her gaze and held it. "First day on the job, and I should be giving you a raise already," he teased.

"No need," she replied, her face taking on a pink color. "I expected to help with other things besides child care when I was hired."

He felt like kicking himself for giving in to the temptation to tease her. It obviously made her uncomfortable. And why shouldn't it? He was her *employer*. He hadn't meant for his comment to come out the way it had, hadn't meant to make it sound so… He ducked his head, wishing he could take the words back. Hell, he wasn't trying to seduce her, so why had he felt the need to tease her in a way that sounded like he was?

She cleared her throat and he looked up at her. "I think everything you need is here," she said.

"You're not joining us?"

She opened the refrigerator and removed a bottle of water. "You and Brayden are used to spending your evenings together, and I've spent all day with him. I think he'd like some one-on-one time with his dad. I'll see Brayden later at bedtime, if that's all right."

He wasn't familiar with the ways of nannies, and he didn't want to pressure her, especially on her first day. "Sure."

He wasn't sure that was right, but what did he know? They'd never had a live-in nanny before. He tried to reason with himself. Why should he care what the woman did, as long as she took good care of his son? And she seemed to be doing that, from what he'd seen.

Brayden continued to play quietly, and Luke decided Hayley was probably right about the two of them needing to spend a little special time together. He'd been so busy all day that he hadn't realized until that moment that he missed sharing most of the day with his son.

Needing some space and a few minutes to clear his head, he joined Brayden again and helped gather up the menagerie of animals and assorted vehicles, surprised that his son helped him with the small chore. His usual style was to turn around and walk away. Luke had learned the hard way that it didn't do any good to yell at the boy. Even at two, Brayden had developed a way to tune out anything he didn't want to hear and had inherited his mother's knack for tantrums. Picking up toys was one of those things that could set Brayden off in a split second. Going to bed was another.

When they finished, Luke took him by the hand, but it was Brayden who pulled Luke to the counter. Luke raised an eyebrow when the little guy pulled a bib from the counter and handed it to him, then lifted his chin without being asked so Luke could hook it behind his neck.

"Looks like you and Hayley had a good day," Luke said, settling Brayden in his seat.

He watched her move around the counter to give Brayden a hug, and he felt even worse. In one day, his son had taken to her and she to him. If Brayden's mother had done the same…

"I'll see you later, Brayden," she said, placing a kiss on the top of the boy's head. She looked at Luke. "Same time in the morning?"

"If it works out for you, yes."

"Then I'll see you at six-thirty with breakfast."

"There's no need—"

"I don't mind at all."

He decided arguing would be useless. "Okay, then."

He watched her walk out of the room, until she'd disappeared. But even after he heard her close the door to her room, he had to force his attention back to his son. His conscience bothered him. He'd been unfair to her from the moment he had seen her getting out of her car that first day. So what if his sister was matchmaking? He didn't have to fall for it. Hayley Brooks was an attractive young woman. He couldn't deny that. But he was old enough—and wise enough—to get past her looks. Or he should be. He had to be. Only a fool who had made the mistake of marrying the wrong woman would let his libido rule his head.

Unfortunately, he hadn't been able to convince his libido that he wasn't attracted to Hayley.

"Hey, Brayden, ready to eat?" he asked. But it didn't keep him from thinking about the woman who was now living in his home.

"LET'S GET YOU CLEANED UP." Hayley took the colored markers from Brayden and lifted him into her arms. "If it warms up enough," she told him, "maybe you can do some finger painting on the patio after lunch. Would you like that?"

"Dat," he echoed.

Laughing, she gave him a hug and carried him through the house and up the stairs to the bathroom on the second floor. In only four days, he had begun to talk more. Of course, it wasn't always clear what he was saying, and he'd suddenly started echoing the last word of everything she said to him. She'd meant to ask Luke if he'd noticed it, but after her first day, she hadn't seen much of him.

As she dampened a washcloth and added a drop of soap, she thought of how little she'd seen of her employer. During the day, he was out of the house, and in the evening, school and studying had kept her busy. "And that's the way it should be," she muttered while washing the bright marks of color from Brayden's hands and arms.

"Shoo bee," Brayden echoed.

She looked at him and laughed. "You're probably right."

"Right about what?"

She jumped at the sound of a much-deeper voice and spun around to find Luke standing in the doorway of the bathroom. "Sorry," he said. "I didn't mean to scare you."

"You only surprised me." She moved to the sink, her heart pounding and her hands trembling from the fright. Rinsing the cloth, she wondered why he'd come inside so early. "Brayden has been coloring with the markers and missed the paper."

"I think there are some crayons in a drawer in his room. His aunt Erin sent him some for his birthday."

Nodding, she returned to Brayden and wiped away the soap. "I'll check. We may try finger painting this afternoon."

Luke reached over and tugged at Brayden's curls. "I bet you'll like that," he told his son.

"Dat," Brayden repeated.

Hayley felt Luke watching her. "I'll make sure he doesn't make a mess. We'll only do it if the weather is nice. Out on the patio."

"Sounds like fun."

She rinsed the washcloth again and placed it over the towel bar to dry. "It sounds messy, I know," she said, turning back to Luke and wishing he would leave. She didn't like having to explain herself to him, but she felt she needed to. "I have an old shirt that had been one of my brothers. It will cover most of Brayden's clothes so the paint won't get on them. And I'll wash down any paint that gets on the patio."

"I'm not worried about it," Luke replied. "Brayden made a lot more messes before you came to watch him, and we both survived them."

Although the bathroom would be considered large by most standards, to Hayley it was too small for comfort. Before she could scoop up Brayden and escape, Luke had taken him by the hand and turned to leave. Hayley breathed a sigh of relief.

"You haven't started lunch yet, have you?" Luke asked as she joined them in the hallway.

"No, not yet. Brayden and I have been busy, and I wanted to get him cleaned up first."

Luke nodded. "Good. I thought we could run into town and have lunch at the café. It's a good place to meet people and get a feel for the town."

"Oh! Well, sure, if you think so. I guess." The suggestion took her by surprise, and she wasn't sure what to think. "Brayden needs his clothes changed, though, and I need to run a brush through my hair and—"

"I'll take care of Brayden, while you do whatever you need to do. We'll meet you in the family room when you're ready."

She nodded and hurried down the stairs to her room. As she freshened her makeup, she realized she was letting things get to her and worrying when she probably had no need to. It wasn't the way she usually reacted to things.

"You're going to a small-town café to eat lunch with your employer and your charge," she whispered to her reflection in the mirror. "There's no reason to panic or be nervous."

Grabbing her purse from her room and slipping on a jacket, she met Luke and Brayden in the family room, just as they were coming down the stairs.

"Are we ready?" Luke asked.

Brayden shouted that he was and Hayley nodded in agreement. Once in the pickup, with Brayden settled in his car seat in the back of the extended cab, they were on their way.

Hayley watched out the window as Luke drove them to town. Others might think it was a bleak scene, but she loved the contrast of dark, bare trees and earthy, dormant fields against the bright blue sky. The late winter had gifted them with warm days, well above freezing, and birds were busy hopping from tree limb to tree limb. Even though she'd lived on a farm while growing up, she'd become accustomed to the city and often forgot the beauty of a world without skyscrapers, interstate highways and traffic.

She kept Brayden busy during the ride by reciting nursery rhymes, which made him giggle and squeal. Luke joined in now and then, and before she knew it, they were almost to town.

"Did you see much of Desperation when you stopped for groceries the other day?" Luke asked.

"Only a little," she admitted. "I was focused more on where I needed to go, since I had Brayden with me and didn't really look around much."

Within seconds, he brought the truck to a stop at the intersection of Main Street and the county road. "We'll be at the Chick-a-Lick before you know it."

She wasn't certain she'd heard right. "Excuse me? The what?"

"Chick-a-Wick!" came the yell from the back.

Luke laughed. "He has a little trouble with some of his letters. It's the Chick-a-Lick Café, and it's been here for as long as I can remember. People have been known to come as far as fifty miles for the food and the company."

"Then I'm definitely looking forward to lunch."

After turning the corner, Luke drove slowly down the street. Pointing out the window, he said, "That's the old Opera House the town folks have been renovating for several years."

"It's beautiful," she answered, as he pulled into a parking spot in front of what was obviously the café. She waited until he shut off the engine, then she stepped out of the truck and took Brayden from his car seat.

Luke joined them at the curb and took the squirming little boy from her arms, setting him on the sidewalk. "He loves coming to the café. He gets to see all his favorite people."

"I guess so," Hayley said, laughing, as Brayden ran toward the café. They followed and Luke opened the door, while Hayley took Brayden's hand in hers, and they all walked inside.

Her first impression was that the Chick-a-Lick was a typical small town café. But when she stepped farther inside, silence moved through the room filled with customers like a wave, and she felt all eyes on her. "Oh, my," she whispered.

Chapter Three

For several seconds, Luke wasn't sure what to do. Everyone in the café was watching them, and the words *fight or flight* jumped to mind. Common sense quickly told him that there would be no tucking tail and retreating. He'd have to find a way to make this uncomfortable moment a little easier for both him and Hayley.

"There's a booth over there," he said, pointing to the only empty spot in the café. Hayley nodded, and he followed her through the crowded but unusually quiet room, making a point to nod and say hello to neighbors and friends.

"Hey, Luke," Tanner O'Brien called to him.

"Tanner," Luke greeted, and smiled at his friend's wife as if walking into the Chick-a-Lick with a pretty woman was a daily thing for him. "Good to see you, Jules. And Wyoming," he added, patting their young son on the shoulder as he passed.

He grabbed a high chair on the way, and by the time Hayley had settled Brayden into it and scooted into one side of the booth, the usual buzz of conversation in the café had resumed. Still, Luke knew people were speculating on who she was and what was going on.

Hayley picked up one of the menus tucked behind

the napkin holder and looked around the room. "You were right. It's definitely a popular place."

He nodded his agreement and grabbed his own menu, hoping to hide the fact that he was clueless on how to handle this predicament he'd gotten them into. He hadn't given any thought to how the first visit to town with Hayley would quickly become a topic of gossip. After all, he'd never come into the café before with any woman other than his wife, when he was married, and everyone in town knew how that had ended.

He rarely missed Saturday lunch at the Chick-a-Lick. Even Brayden knew with some kind of sixth sense where they were going when they started for town on Saturday. Leaving Brayden behind was never an option. His son would complain. Loudly. But taking Brayden, while leaving Hayley behind, just hadn't seemed right, either. So here they were.

As he looked over the menu, he told himself that she deserved to have a meal she hadn't cooked, and this was the perfect chance to introduce her around so she could meet people and maybe make a few friends. Now all he had to do was find a way to keep gossip at a minimum.

By the pale, pink blotches on Hayley's cheeks, he guessed she was feeling a little embarrassed and maybe even uncomfortable. "They're curious," he told her. "They're all good people."

"It's all right," she answered. "I guess I'd be surprised if they weren't. I'm sure that even if I was eighty and gray-haired and wrinkled, they'd still wonder."

He couldn't help but laugh. "Yeah, you're right." And he felt better because she understood.

"So what's good?" she asked. "Besides everything."

Suddenly glad she wasn't eighty, gray-haired and wrinkled, he was in the middle of making lunch suggestions when the waitress came to the table.

"Hey, Luke," she greeted. Placing several packages of crackers on the table in front of Brayden, she turned to smile at Hayley. "I'm Darla. Welcome to the Chick-a-Lick."

"Nice to meet you, Darla. I'm Hayley Brooks, Brayden's new nanny."

Darla took the hand she offered. "Aren't you the lucky one? He's such a cute little guy. So are you all ready to order?"

When Hayley nodded in his direction, he answered, "I guess we are," and they gave Darla their orders. She'd just walked away when Tanner and Jules O'Brien approached the booth with their son.

"Okay, I'll say it. Jules is dying of curiosity," Tanner said, laughing.

"I am not!" His wife gave him a playful punch in the arm, and then laughed, too. "All right, I guess small-town nosiness has rubbed off on me," she said, smiling at Hayley.

Luke hurried to introduce his friends, and explained that Hayley was his son's new nanny, without feeling it was the wrong thing to say.

"Perfect," Jules said, with a glance at her husband.

"Hi there, Wyoming," Hayley said to their son. "How old are you?"

Wyoming held up three fingers.

"He'll be four in August," Jules added. "And we really should get home. It's so nice to meet you, Hayley. I hope you'll all stop by the ranch sometime."

They said their goodbyes, and when the O'Briens were gone, Luke let out a sigh. "I guess that went okay, didn't it?"

"Very okay," Hayley replied.

Darla soon returned with their meal, and the three of them fell silent as they enjoyed it. Luke didn't fail to notice that Hayley kept an eye on Brayden, helping him with his food the way a mother would. And for a change, Brayden behaved like a perfect little gentleman, instead of wanting to get up to run around the café.

Luke had just finished paying the bill at the cash register and they were ready to leave, when the door opened. "Looks like you both have your hands full," Luke told the couple who walked into the café.

"Double trouble," Dusty McPherson replied, glancing at his wife with a grin, as he jiggled one of his twin sons in his arms. More quietly he said, "Hey, Luke, I've been meaning to ask where Dylan has disappeared to."

Luke shrugged and kept his voice low, too. "He just said he needed to get away." After glancing around to make sure no one was listening, he continued. "You know how it is with him this time of year."

"Maybe he'll be able to sort it all out if he's away from the ranch," Dusty suggested. "Sometimes just getting away can help. I know it did me. Why, if it hadn't been—"

"Dusty," his wife warned, as she shifted the other twin in her arms. There was a sparkle in her eyes as she glanced at Hayley with a smile. "I'm sure Luke and his friend aren't interested."

Dusty grinned at Hayley. "Right. Beg your pardon, ma'am."

Hayley laughed. "None needed. I'm Hayley Brooks. Brayden's new nanny."

"A nanny!" Kate looked pointedly at her husband and frowned. "Now why didn't you think of that?"

He slipped an arm around his wife's waist. "Maybe after the next one…or two?" he suggested with a bawdy wink.

Laughing, Luke moved to the door. "I'll tell Dylan to stop by when he gets back. Maybe you can talk some sense into him, if he hasn't managed to find some on his own."

"In the meantime," Kate said, placing a hand on Hayley's arm, "I'm Kate McPherson, and if you decide Luke is a slave driver, I'm sure I can find a position for you. If you get my drift. Oh, and this cowboy is my husband, Dusty." Before moving on, she flashed Luke a smug smile.

"Wow, what a pair!" Hayley said, as they exited the café and started for the pickup. "And what nice friends you have. They went out of their way to make me feel welcome."

Luke shrugged as he opened the truck door for her. "Like I said, people in Desperation are nice folks." When they'd settled in the truck and were on their way back to the ranch, he turned to look at her. "You don't have to worry now. Everybody in town will know you're Brayden's new nanny before the sun goes down."

"I guess that's a good thing," she replied. "But I

wasn't really worried. I try not to pay a lot of attention to what others say, especially when they don't know the circumstances. Still, for you and Brayden, I'm glad everyone will know."

He was surprised at her honesty and unsure of how to answer, so he nodded in agreement before concentrating on the road ahead. It was pretty clear that she wasn't the type to keep her opinions to herself. While that might have been a problem with others—his ex-wife, for instance—with Hayley he was beginning to appreciate it. He never felt she was being unkind, and her honesty made things easier. He wouldn't have to wonder where he stood with her. Even the live-in situation wasn't proving to be the problem he'd expected it would be, now that they were falling into a routine. And he was hoping that time would take care of the attraction he felt for her. Not that it had, so far.

As he turned into the driveway to the ranch, he glanced in the rearview mirror at his son, who had fallen asleep. Brayden had been unnaturally good all afternoon, and Luke could only chalk that up to Hayley's influence. He admitted to himself that he was pleased she hadn't given up and left that first day of the interview.

"I'll take Brayden up to bed," he told her, as he pulled up to the house and shut off the engine.

"Thanks," she said, sliding out of the truck. "It's amazing how heavy something so small can sometimes be."

After putting Brayden in his bed, Luke found Hayley sitting in the kitchen, her head down as she turned the page of the book in front of her. He cleared his throat to keep from frightening her, and when she looked up, he spoke. "I've got some work to do out in the machine shed. If you need me, just give a shout."

She nodded, but immediately went back to whatever she was reading. By the size of the book, he suspected it was for school.

Once in the shed, he felt more like himself. Lunch with Hayley at the café hadn't been what he'd expected, and he was grateful for work that took his mind off it.

"How's it goin'?"

Luke jumped at the sound of the voice and dropped the crowbar he was using, missing his right foot by inches. "Damn, Dylan!" he shouted at the sight of his older brother. "You might try warning a person instead of sneaking up on him."

Dylan snorted. "You might try being a bit less jumpy."

Picking up the crowbar, Luke set it against the feed mixer he'd been working on and wiped his hands on his jeans, doing his best to keep his temper in check. "I've had a lot on my mind, what with you running off and leaving the ranching to me. Add that I didn't expect you back for another week, and I sure wasn't ready for somebody to come sneaking up on me."

"Okay, okay," Dylan said, scowling. "Next time I'll come whistling a tune."

Luke recognized his brother's mood and knew better than to push it. Stuffing his hands in the pockets of his jeans, he leaned against the mixer. "Did you see Erin?"

Dylan shook his head and joined his brother, leaning his hip against the machine. "Nope. I didn't make it that far. I got as far as Dallas, spent a few nights in a motel and decided that leaving you with all the work isn't fair."

"I've always managed okay."

"I never figured you couldn't."

Luke could see the worry in his brother's dark eyes, but he suspected it didn't have anything to do with how he'd managed with the ranch. "Wanna talk about it?" he asked, prepared for a blast of mind-your-own-business from Dylan.

Shoving away from the mixer, Dylan shook his head. "Nah. Nothing to talk about."

Luke watched his brother walk away, but couldn't let him go. "Why don't you stay for supper?" he called to him. "There's usually plenty."

Dylan turned back. "Plenty? I've never known you to keep anything more than the makings for a couple of peanut butter and jelly sandwiches and a few cans of beer in the fridge."

"Hayley always makes a big supper."

One dark eyebrow arched above Dylan's eye. "Hayley?"

"Brayden's nanny."

"So you hired her, huh?"

Luke shrugged. "It wasn't like I had a choice."

"I guess you're right."

"So you'll stay for supper?"

Dylan shook his head. "Not tonight. Maybe another time."

Luke knew better than to insist. "Typical Dylan," he muttered under his breath as he watched his brother leave the building. Dylan was a grown-up, and Luke knew he shouldn't worry, but he did. He'd hoped his brother might come home a changed man, but that was asking too much. At least he was home again, and that would ease the workload. It would also mean there'd be more time spent with Hayley around, and Luke knew that wasn't necessarily a good thing.

HAYLEY LEANED BACK in her chair, stretching her arms above her head, and smiled to herself, thinking of how, in just one week, she and Brayden—and even Luke—had fallen into a comfortable schedule. With Brayden still sleeping since they'd arrived home from lunch at the café, she had to admit that she enjoyed his nap time as much as a mother would. It was her quiet time of the day, when she could clean up the kitchen, straighten the clutter from playtime or concentrate on her studies, without interruption.

But her alone time was shattered when she looked up to see Luke walk into the family room, through the sliding glass door that led to the deck. "Is something wrong?" she asked, when he turned to silently stare out the glass.

He turned to look at her. "No, I don't think so."

She marked her place and closed her book. "You don't sound convinced."

He stared outside at the deck again. "My brother is back, but I don't know if that's good or bad," he said, more to himself than to her.

"Seems to me it would be good," she answered.

Luke turned to look at her again, his face set in a deep, worried frown. "I'm not sure. Something is wrong and has been for a long time. I just wish I knew what."

She folded her hands in front of her. "Why don't you ask him?"

Luke snorted. "Ask him? Sure, if I want him to bite off my head."

She shrugged and stood, moving to the sink, her back to him. "What makes you think that?"

"You have to know Dylan. He's… He's broody. And that's normal for him. But lately he's just been— I don't know."

She turned on the faucet to fill a glass of water, and replied, "I guess you'd know that better than me."

"You'd think so, wouldn't you?"

He sounded a little bewildered. And close. Without turning around, she cleared her throat. "And that's a bad thing, why?"

"It just isn't Dylan, that's all. You'd probably have to know where he's coming from to understand."

She felt more than heard him move away and relaxed. Shutting off the water, she began putting a few odds and ends in the dishwasher, then closed the door to it before turning to look at him. "What do you mean? Coming from where?" She didn't miss his frown. "Or maybe I shouldn't be asking."

He shook his head as he walked back to the sliding door. "It's a long story."

"I have time, if you want to share. Sometimes it helps just to talk it out."

Luke's sigh was heavy with worry. "I wish Dylan would talk it out or at least try. I don't know exactly what it is, but he's been like this for a long time. This year, he's been more quiet than usual. He's always been quiet, but…" He turned to look at her. "I guess that sounds pretty crazy."

"Not really." She returned to her seat and waited, wondering if it might be better to let this go. After all, it wasn't her problem, except that what affected her employer might also affect her and her job. She chose her words carefully. "Everybody reacts to things differently. Obviously something about him has you concerned. While others might not notice, for someone who knows him well, any small shift in his usual behavior would bring up a red flag." She looked up to see him studying her.

"You're pretty smart, you know that?"

She felt her face heat with embarrassment. "Not really, but I've taken some psych classes. And growing up in a big family gave me a little personal insight."

"I'll bet it did."

She didn't know if she could help him with his brother, but she hoped she could. From her own experiences, she knew that, in a family, one person's mood often affected others. "There are three of you in the family?" she asked.

He nodded and joined her at the counter. "Erin is the oldest, then Dylan, then me. Our folks—" He avoided looking at her and ran his hand through his hair. "Well, that's part of the story, I guess."

"Aunt Rita said you lost your folks in an accident when you were in high school."

"I was fifteen."

It was clear that he still carried a lot of emotional pain from his parents' deaths. She knew she'd been lucky. Everyone in her family was alive and fairly well, except for the usual ranching-related broken bones and cuts along the way. Her younger brother had been in a car accident two years before and her father had suffered a stroke the year before that, but as a whole, they were all doing well.

"That must have been hard. For all of you," she said quietly.

"Yeah. But it was hardest on Dylan. He still takes time off every year near the anniversary of when it happened." He clasped his hands on the table in front of him and looked at her. "He was a senior and captain of the baseball team, so he left early for the first game of the season. The game was canceled though, when a storm moved in, but by the time they thought the storm had passed, Dylan hadn't come home. He was usually pretty responsible about that sort of thing. When they didn't hear from him, they went to look for him. They didn't know that a second storm behind the first was even worse. The rain was so bad, they could barely see the road, and they were broadsided by a semitruck."

Hayley's throat constricted with emotion. "I can't even imagine what it was like for you all."

"The phone lines were down in town, so Dylan had stayed at the school with a few friends, waiting out both storms. When the rain began to let up, he started home and came upon the accident, just as the emergency crews arrived."

"Oh, no," she whispered, imagining how Luke's brother must have felt.

He looked up at her. "He's never gotten over it, and he refuses to talk about it. He quit the baseball team and devoted himself to the ranch and to finishing school.

He'd been offered a college scholarship, but wouldn't take it, and nothing anyone said could change it. Erin stayed around and took care of us both, until I graduated, then she started traveling the rodeo circuit full-time."

"Aunt Rita mentioned she's a barrel racer."

They sat in silence for a few minutes, until Luke pushed away from the table and stood. "I ought to drive over to Dylan's and make sure he's doing okay."

"And I need to check on Brayden." Hayley stood, unsure of whether to say something about what he had shared with her or to just let it go.

"Wait a second," he said. "What with all this stuff about Dylan, I forgot something. Let me get my checkbook and I'll pay you for this week, before I go."

His words were a reminder to her that she was supposed to be doing her job, not telling her employer how to deal with his brother. She was there to take care of his son. She obviously had a problem, but Luke wasn't it. She was. Hadn't she spent the past five days denying her attraction to him? And wasn't that beyond foolish of her? Especially since she wasn't interested in a relationship with anyone. Not after Nathan and definitely not at this point in her life.

While she silently scolded herself, Luke returned to the room, holding a check in his hand. "You're great, Hayley," he said. "With Brayden," he added quickly.

For a reason she didn't want to explore, disappointment hit her. Swallowing a sigh, she turned to leave. But a hand on her arm stopped her and she turned back.

"Look, I'm sorry," Luke said. "I guess I don't know how to handle this kind of situation." He released her and raked his hand through his hair. "It's just been Brayden and me for so long, and having you here, taking care of him— Well, it's changed a lot of things. I guess I'm just having trouble..."

"Adjusting?"

A smile lit his face. "That'd be the word."

Her heart skipped a beat and without thinking, she took a step forward. "That makes two of us."

His eyes darkened as he looked at her. "We're a couple of misfits, I guess."

His voice was husky, sending a shiver of warmth through her, until she realized what was happening. Giving herself a hard, mental shake, she stepped back immediately. Was she crazy?

"You—you'd better get going," she managed to say. Clutching the paycheck in her hand, she brushed past him, headed for her room. If she wasn't careful, she'd have to quit her job. And she'd have no one to blame but herself.

"SORRY ABOUT THE INTERRUPTION," Dylan told Hayley that evening, "but I need to get these cattle records. I'm glad I got to see Brayden before bedtime, though. Makes me wish I had a little one so I'd need somebody like you to look after him."

Luke opened his mouth to tell his brother that Hayley was already taken, but he stopped and clamped it shut. One or the other of them would take it wrong, when all he meant was— He didn't mean anything. Not a damn thing, and if his brother wanted to start up with her, he wasn't going to stop him. After all, she was his son's nanny, not some woman he had a thing for.

Hayley shrugged. "I grew up the only girl in a family of five kids. My mom needed help, so I was the one to do it. In fact, as soon as I was old enough to put a knife, fork and spoon on the table, I was in the kitchen."

"Nothing like Erin, right, Luke?" Dylan asked.

Luke thought about his sister, whose skills leaned more toward horses than cooking. Way more. "Erin has her own talents," he reminded his brother.

Hayley helped Brayden down from his high chair and looked at Luke. "Not every woman enjoys cooking."

"Or being a mother," Dylan said. He immediately ducked his head and glanced at his brother. "Sorry, I didn't mean—"

"Forget it," Luke answered, brushing off the comment, and stood. He knew Dylan had been as taken in by Kendra as he had. Erin, too.

Taking Brayden by the hand, Hayley turned to them both. "Cooking and nurturing aren't for women only, you know," she said, then hurried past them.

Luke watched her take Brayden from the room, unsure of what to say.

Dylan took a step in the same direction. "She seemed kind of upset. Maybe I should apologize."

"Leave her alone for a few minutes. She'll cool down, and I'll go make sure everything is okay."

Dylan's expression was repentant. "Look, I'm sorry. I didn't mean to hurt her feelings or whatever. I just— I guess I should've kept my mouth shut, but I was trying to compliment her." He turned to look in the direction where she'd disappeared. "I sure blew that, didn't I?"

Luke approached him and put a hand on his shoulder. "Don't worry about it. She has an independent streak."

"Like Erin."

Luke had to smile. "In a way, yeah, I guess. Don't let it bother you. She'll be fine."

But he wasn't convinced she would and he didn't stay around to explain it to his brother. The evening had been pleasant, but he'd felt a reserve about Hayley that had bothered him. Whatever had caused it, he knew he should probably find out so he wouldn't repeat it. This nanny thing was new to him, and he wasn't sure what was expected of him.

He found her upstairs in his son's bedroom. As he stood, watching from the doorway, she pulled out a small pair of pajamas from the bureau drawer. Placing them on the bed, she bent to give Brayden a hug.

"Bath time," she announced, "and then you can get in your clean jammies."

"No," Brayden said, running to hide behind the closet door.

She didn't say anything for several seconds, until Brayden peeked out at her. "Maybe your daddy will let you go back down to tell your uncle Dylan good night. Would you like that?"

Brayden stepped out from behind the door, bobbing his head in an eager nod.

Luke cleared his throat so he wouldn't spook her. "Go on down then."

The look of joy on his young son's face was priceless as the boy sped past him out the door. "Slow down on the stairs, Brayden," he called to him. "We'll be there in a minute."

Hayley got to her feet. "The button is loose on these pajamas. I have a needle and thread in my room."

Nodding, Luke followed her into the hallway. "He was excited to see Dylan this evening. I didn't realize my brother was so important to him."

"It just goes to show how important family is," she said over her shoulder as they walked down the stairs. "Sometimes we don't realize how much until something happens to remind us."

She went on to her room, but when he heard strange noises coming from there only seconds later, he went to check. He found her pulling and pounding on the bureau drawer, which apparently was stuck.

"Here, let me," he said, stepping up beside her. "I should've remembered that it never did fit right." Wiggling the drawer just right, he slid it open. "There."

"I can usually get it," she said and moved aside.

"Wait." He touched her arm, stopping her. He could tell by her tone and the way her chin tilted up that she was still a little put off by his brother's earlier comment. "Dylan didn't mean anything, you know. I don't know what got into him."

She nodded, slowly. "I know you're concerned about him." She sighed and looked down. "I shouldn't have let it get to me."

Placing his finger under her chin, he lifted it until he could see her face. He didn't want to talk about his brother. He didn't want to see her this way. "Why don't we all forget about it?" he suggested, staring down into her bright blue eyes. She nodded again, but he didn't pull his hand away. She didn't move away, either, and he couldn't seem to stop himself from leaning even closer. Before he knew it, his lips were on hers.

"Hey, Luke, where are you? Brayden wants—"

Hayley jerked back even more quickly than Luke did at the sound of Dylan's voice.

In the doorway, Dylan stood, looking embarrassed. "Uh, I didn't mean to—"

"I need to get Brayden to bed." Hayley crossed the room and brushed past Dylan, hurrying from the room.

The two men silently stared after her. Luke wasn't sure what to say. He hadn't planned to kiss her. It had just…happened.

Clearing his throat, Dylan shifted from one foot to the other. "Brayden wants a cookie. I didn't know you were— I wasn't sure where to find them."

Luke commanded his voice to work. "Maybe now isn't the best time."

He could hear Hayley talking to Brayden as she took him upstairs. He'd sure managed to make a mess of things, and he could only imagine what his brother thought. But he wasn't about to say anything. It was possible Dylan hadn't seen anything. After all, not much had happened. Disappointment washed over him, and he lowered himself to the edge of her bed.

Now what?

Chapter Four

Hayley's hands were still trembling as she tucked Brayden into bed after his bath, and she prayed that the little boy hadn't seen or heard anything that had happened. "Good night, Brayden," she told him, kissing his forehead.

His reply was a smile as his eyes slowly closed, his thick eyelashes coming to rest on velvety cheeks. He was a beautiful child, she thought, as she watched to make sure he was sleeping soundly. Just looking at him reminded her of his father, and she felt her face heat with shame that she hadn't done anything to stop Luke from kissing her and in fact had encouraged it without meaning to. Not that she'd known it was going to happen, and she suspected from the look on his face that he hadn't, either.

The house was eerily quiet as she walked downstairs to her room. Instead of turning on the light, she dressed in the dark, slipped into her pajamas and crawled into bed, determined to fall asleep quickly.

She didn't.

In spite of trying not to think about what had happened with her employer earlier, her mind was filled with it. Even worse, if she dared to be truthful, she'd have to admit she'd enjoyed it. Far too much. Especially for something that had been so very, very brief.

Though she warred with herself, she soon fell asleep, only to be awakened later by the sound of thunder. That was soon followed by what seemed to be hail hitting her window. Because the sky was beginning to lighten and she obviously wasn't going to sleep well, she reluctantly decided to start the day, not at all sure how it would play out.

She'd put a load of Brayden's play clothes in the washing machine and was heading back to the kitchen, when she heard someone descending the stairs. Instead of stopping as she usually would have done to greet Luke, she hurried on, making sure she was busy and had her back to him when he approached the kitchen. She knew she was being foolish, but she couldn't even imagine making eye contact with him. Not yet.

"I'll grab some coffee later," Luke said from somewhere behind her. "The weatherman says there's danger of some of the creeks flooding, so we need to get the cattle moved, just in case."

She sensed it wasn't the only thing bothering him, since he hadn't made eye contact with her, either. "I'll fill a thermos with coffee for both you and Dylan."

"You don't have to do that. You're Brayden's nanny not—"

"I'm offering," she insisted. "Never look a gift horse in the mouth."

She smiled as she glanced up at him and wished she'd said nothing. He was looking directly at her mouth.

He made a choking sound and ducked his head.

When he looked up again, it was to glance out the sliding doors. "I'll hunt down my rain gear and be back for the coffee."

When he'd left the room, the last thing she wanted to do was think about the conversation they'd just had. Turning on the radio beneath the cabinets, she hoped the news, if not the music, would distract her thoughts, at least until Luke left to do chores.

The thermos was filled and ready when he returned. Doing her best to pretend nothing had happened—and never would—she leaned over the counter to hand it to him.

At that moment, their gazes met, and she couldn't force herself to look away. There was something in his eyes.... Contrition? The same embarrassment she was feeling? Whatever it was, they were both very careful when he took the paper bag from her.

"Tell Dylan he's welcome to join us for lunch," she said, when they'd both taken a step back.

"I will."

He turned around without looking her way, and she watched as he strode through the family room to the door that led to the garage. She hadn't expected to feel the relief that swept through her. She should've known that he would be as embarrassed about what had happened as she'd been. If she'd thought there might be a problem with falling for her employer—or he for her—when she'd applied for the job, she wouldn't have accepted it in the first place. Besides, she told herself, there really wasn't a problem, unless either of them made that regretful incidence into one, or repeated it.

She knew she wasn't going to. She suspected he wasn't, either.

The rest of her morning was filled with Brayden, who was raring to go the second he jumped out of bed. For a little boy who'd hidden behind his daddy, barely a week before, he'd definitely come out of his shell quickly.

"Want jooze!" he shouted, as he stopped scribbling on the pad of paper Hayley had given him.

Looking over her shoulder at him, she reached for a plastic cup in the cabinet. "Only a little juice," she told him. "And you need to sit in your chair to drink it."

He shook his head, and his lower lip jutted out. "No."

She laughed at herself for thinking only a few days ago that he might be one of the few two-year-olds who wouldn't go through what was known to mothers around the world as The Terrible Twos. She'd obviously been dreaming.

"Climb into your chair, Brayden, and I'll give you your juice."

"No."

Without replying, she replaced the pitcher of juice she'd pulled from the refrigerator. Arguing with a two-year-old was foolish, at best, but she also wanted him to understand that rules were rules. It was something she'd noticed his father was lax about. Brayden was a sweet little boy, and all he needed were a few simple boundaries.

"Want joo-o-o-ze!"

The shriek caused her to jump, but before she could respond, a male voice replied, "What's wrong, buddy?"

She looked up to see Luke enter the room, and she

quickly explained. "He's voicing his disagreement about sitting in his chair while drinking his juice."

Luke leaned down and picked up his son, swinging Brayden up to settle the little boy on his shoulders. "Do what Hayley says, buddy, so you can have your juice."

Hayley ignored how her body had reacted with a ripple when she'd heard his voice, and now she tensed in anticipation of more of the same. In spite of her determination not to let what had happened cause any more problems, she didn't seem to be able to carry through with it.

"I'll be right back," he told his son. "I have to get something for Uncle Dylan."

She hated the feeling of relief she felt when he disappeared. Somehow she'd have to find a comfort zone where she felt safe and could deal with the turmoil that being around him was causing. Oh, she'd been aware of Luke from the moment they'd met, but she hadn't worried about it. After his initial aversion to hiring her, it seemed they'd come to a mutual place in their relationship that was comfortable. Boy, had she been wrong.

When Luke returned, he lifted his son into his seat, and she immediately poured Brayden's juice. When she placed the cup in front of him, it sloshed when he hurried to pick it up, but she simply smiled. Little messes were expected.

Luke sat at the counter next to Brayden, looking through a booklet of some kind. Tension made the air heavy, but Hayley didn't know what to do to lighten it.

"Down," Brayden shouted, when his juice was gone.

Luke chuckled and was helping his son down from the chair when Dylan walked in through the sliding doors. "I forgot to mention that Dylan would be here," Luke explained.

Dylan nodded in greeting to Hayley, then walked to stand by Luke. "We'll just have to wait until the rain stops to do anything else."

Luke nodded. "At least the cattle are moved, so that's one less worry."

"And fed," Dylan added, "but we'd better plan to take some hay out this evening, or we'll be wishing tomorrow that we had."

"Maybe we need to sit down and figure out what else we need to do if this keeps up."

"Good idea." Dylan started to move away, but stopped. "Sorry. I forgot that spare room is in use now."

Hayley felt his gaze on her and prayed that he didn't notice her embarrassment. "Give me a couple of minutes, and you can work here."

She quickly cleared the countertop of Brayden's crayons, then she reached into a drawer near the phone and pulled out a pad of paper and two pens, placing them on the counter. Without a word, she moved out of the kitchen and walked past both men to where Brayden was playing quietly at the far end of the room with his toys.

"Let's take your toys upstairs," she said, reaching her hand down to him.

"No."

Her heart sank. Of all the times she needed him to be cooperative, he had to choose that moment to be contrary. Now, not only would Luke be around most of the day, but his brother—who she was convinced had been a witness to the incident—would be, too.

"He's okay," Luke said from behind her. "We'll keep an eye on him. We've done it plenty of times before. As long as he's playing, it isn't a problem."

She opened her mouth to argue, but suspected to do so would be inviting more trouble. "If you say so." She wondered if she should thank him, but thought better of it. "I'll be in my room. He'll probably be ready for a nap before too long, so when he starts getting grumpy or tired, just let me know."

Both men assured her that they would, so she escaped to her room. Once there, she couldn't enjoy her alone time. Relaxing was out of the question, and all she could think about was that she wasn't doing her job. Finally, she scolded herself for wasting the gift of private time she'd been given and settled on the bed, where she opened the book she'd been trying to read.

Sometime later, she opened her eyes, shocked and ashamed that she'd fallen asleep. A quick look at her watch told her she'd slept much longer than she should have, and she wondered why no one had tried to wake her. After checking her hair in the mirror to make sure she wasn't a mess, she hurried out to the family room, in a panic that she'd find Luke and Dylan gone, Brayden alone and the house a disaster. Instead, the two men were watching television, Brayden nowhere to be seen, and the room as neat as it had been earlier.

"Um, where's Brayden?" she asked, her voice a sleepy croak.

They both turned to look at her. "He fell asleep, so I took him up to bed," Luke answered.

Her panic increased. "Then he's been asleep—"

"No," he said, shaking his head and glancing at his

brother. "It was a short nap, then we all had a bite to eat, and I put him to bed for the night about fifteen minutes ago."

When his attention returned to the television, she didn't know what to think or what to say. "I'm sorry, I should have—"

"Look," he said, getting to his feet, "we never discussed your days off, and you haven't had one in over a week. When it comes to Brayden, I've taken care of him for the past year and a half on my own. An afternoon and evening isn't going to kill me." He looked at his brother, and then turned back to her with a smile. "Or him."

"Maybe I should go check on him."

"No need. I'll do it. This is officially your half day off. Go do whatever you want to do." He started to walk away, but turned back. "The only thing is, with all this rain, I wouldn't try to drive anywhere."

"Oh, of course not," she answered, completely bewildered.

When he was gone, she went to the kitchen, still embarrassed that she'd fallen asleep and shirked her nanny duties.

"Don't worry about it."

She spun around to discover Dylan standing on the other side of the counter. Opening her mouth to reply, she realized she had nothing to say.

"He isn't mad at you," he said. "We all need some time off. Some of us more than others."

"I guess we do," she admitted, and decided then and there to put worries of her long nap behind her.

"And in case you're wondering," he continued, "if anyone asks, I didn't see anything."

"You...*what?*"

"Yesterday. I didn't see anything. Not anything you should be upset or embarrassed about, I mean. Something like that is kind of...natural, I guess. And my brother deserves good stuff, after what he's been through."

Hayley wasn't sure how to answer. Obviously Dylan had witnessed Luke kissing her. And just as obviously he had taken it the wrong way. Quitting her job would be the right thing to do, considering. But she needed the money for school so she could finish her degree. Without it, finishing wouldn't only be difficult, it might prove impossible.

No, she couldn't quit. She'd have to find a way to get beyond the kiss she'd shared with her employer.

"SO WHAT HAPPENED AFTER I left?" Dylan asked.

Luke kept his attention on dumping feed in the long trough where they were working at Dylan's place. He knew exactly what his brother was getting at, but he'd hoped the subject wouldn't come up between them. "I don't know what you're talking about."

"With Hayley," Dylan supplied.

"Nothing."

"Nothing? Damn, Luke, the air fairly sizzles when the two of you are in the same room."

Luke looked at him out of the corner of his eye. "You're imagining things."

There was a short moment of silence before Dylan answered. "Am I?"

Luke bit the inside of his cheek to keep from groaning. This was becoming more serious than he'd imagined. "Yeah, you are," he finally managed to answer. "There's nothing going on between us, and definitely not on my end."

"So *she* grabbed *you* and kissed you the other night?"

"Damn it!" Luke tossed the empty feed bucket to the ground, where it bounced twice and then rolled to settle in the mud. "It was a crazy thing to do. I don't know what came over me. It happened before I knew what I was doing."

"And you don't regret it, do you?"

The groan slipped out before he could stop it this time. Luke leaned against the side of the barn, the damp wood feeling cool beneath his work jacket. "Yeah, I do, because it's changed everything. I know I shouldn't have done it. But the worst part is, she's been acting like I have the plague or something."

"Give her some time."

Luke looked up at him. "And how do you know this?"

Dylan ducked his head. "I guess I don't. At least not from personal experience."

Sighing, Luke pushed away from the barn. "But I do have experience and should know better."

"If it's bothering you that much—and her, too—maybe if you apologized…"

"But I'm not all that sorry," Luke admitted. "And she might be able to see through it, if I tried to lie. No, the best thing to do is to just let time take care of it."

"Sounds like a plan to me."

"Yeah, that and avoiding her as much as possible, at least for a while."

"Not so easy to do."

Luke blew out a long breath of air. "No kidding? I guess I can always hide out here at your place."

It wasn't as if Luke had to look for extra work to keep him from having to return home too early. The amount of rain the day before alone meant more chores. Those added to the usual ones meant they had their hands full.

They worked until early evening. "Maybe you should just talk to her," Dylan said, as they sat on the porch of the house where they'd grown up. "Get it all out in the open."

Luke shook his head. "I can't risk losing her." When Dylan turned to look at him, one eyebrow raised, Luke hurried on. "Finding someone else to take care of Brayden would be hard enough. Finding someone who does it as well as she does would be impossible."

"But she seems like a reasonable person—"

"She's a woman."

"Yeah, I guess you're right. And considering how little I know about that kind of thing, I'm sure not the one to be giving advice."

Surprised at what Dylan just said, Luke had to hunt for the right words. "There's nothing wrong with your advice," he assured his brother. "And the right woman is out there for you. Somewhere. Count on it."

Dylan nodded, but said nothing else, and Luke knew it was time to go and face the music. Maybe Hayley would have had enough time to either forget that he'd kissed her or least not be so darned jumpy about it. By the time he reached home, he'd almost convinced himself that all would be well, if he'd just pretend nothing had happened.

But when he stepped into the house, Hayley was waiting in the family room, her arms crossed in front of her, and a scowl on her face. He was definitely in trouble for something.

"What did I do?" he asked.

HAYLEY HAD SPENT the past half hour waiting for Luke to return so she could leave for her class. Now that he was finally home, she was so angry, she was almost speechless, as she watched him peel off his jacket and then stand in front of her as if he was completely innocent of everything.

"You really don't know, do you?" she asked.

"Would I be asking if I did?"

Grabbing her big bag, she slung the strap over her shoulder. "Do you remember me telling you the very first day that I had classes that I absolutely couldn't miss on Mondays, Wednesday and Friday evenings, and that I'd have to leave by six o'clock?"

The color drained from his face. "It's Wednesday."

"Yes, it is. And it's almost six-thirty. I'm going to be late for class."

"Hayley, I'm sorry. There's no excuse. I didn't think about it. But it isn't like you'll be locked out of the classroom or anything, is it?"

She felt like crying. Or hitting something. But she did neither. "Being sorry isn't going to make up for the class time I'll miss, and I can assure you that my grade for tonight will reflect my tardiness. All because you forgot."

Color flooded back into his face, which was now tinged with red. "You should've reminded me."

"How?" she asked, before turning for the door.

"Called to remind me, maybe?"

She walked to the table next to the sofa and picked up something from the floor, then returned to stand in front of him. "I tried that," she said, handing him his cell phone. Then she continued to the door.

"I didn't do this on purpose."

She didn't bother to turn around. She'd learned the hard way from Nathan that there were men who thought their careers were more important than any woman's. She'd hoped Luke was different. Apparently she'd been wrong.

"Of course you didn't," she replied. "I never thought you did. But one thing I've learned is that some men can be inconsiderate of women's schedules, if they don't agree with or like what they're doing."

"Now wait just a minute—"

"I don't have a minute," she said, her eyes filling with tears. But even though she didn't have the time to explain, she couldn't stop herself. At the door that led to the garage, she turned to face him. "You don't seem to understand how much my education means to me. And it's possible that no matter what I say, you never will. I've worked long and hard to get as far as I have, and nothing is going to stop me."

"Did I say I wanted to?"

Ignoring what she believed was a question used only to bring attention to him and his feelings, she continued. "This job is helping me finish the last step in a dream I've had for several years. That dream is to be a licensed physician's assistant. That's what I've been working toward, and it's finally within my reach. College is expensive. For that reason, I don't want to lose this job, and I sure don't want to have to quit. But if it's going to be a problem for me to get to my classes on time each week, then maybe it would be better if you find someone else to care for Brayden."

"No, that won't be necessary," he insisted. "I'll do whatever it takes to make sure you're on your way in plenty of time to get to your class on Mondays, Wednesdays and Fridays."

She didn't doubt his sincerity, but she couldn't risk being late for another class or, heaven forbid, missing one. The thought of doing so sent terror through her. All her work and study would be for nothing. If she failed this class this semester, she would have to retake it. In addition to having to set aside another semester of time, there was the financial factor. She just couldn't afford to take the class again.

"I'm finishing my clinicals," she explained. "I can't make up this time. So I just don't think I can risk it."

She turned for the door and was opening it, but he'd reached around and closed it. "You can't quit."

All she wanted to do was climb in her car and drive away so she could get to her class, even if she was going to be late. "Please let go of the door."

He hesitated, but the moment he did remove his hand from the door, Brayden's loud wail filled the small space and bounced off the walls, causing Hayley's ears to ring.

He'd heard her. He might not understand what she'd said, but he did understand the tone of her voice.

"Brayden, honey," she began, but Luke pushed her through the door he'd opened.

"Go!" he told her. "Get to your class. I'll take care of Brayden."

"But—"

"Don't say anything else. It'll only make it worse. Go on. Get out. We'll talk about this later."

Once she was through the door and standing on the cement floor of the garage, the door slammed shut. Beyond it, she could hear Brayden's wailing, and imagined the tears that were falling. Of course she couldn't leave him. But there would have to be some changes made, and they would be on her terms.

Chapter Five

Luke didn't close the door until he was sure Hayley had backed out of the garage and he could hear the car turn onto the road. Only then did he let himself think.

Behind him, the house was quiet. He wasn't sure when the wailing had stopped, but at some point it had been replaced by Brayden's tearful sniffs. Looking down, he saw his son staring up at him with huge, round eyes. Small but chubby arms held his legs in a tight grip. Luke leaned down and picked up his son, holding him close. "It's okay, Brayden. It'll be all right."

But the boy struggled in his arms, and Luke realized he was reaching for the door. "No," Brayden said, hitting the door with his hand. "No go."

"She'll be back later." At least Luke hoped she would. There was no telling how much damage he'd caused by not being home on time and making her late for her class. He hadn't exactly been nice, either. She had every right to be angry.

Glancing at his watch, he was reminded that he had a long evening ahead, waiting and wondering what would happen. Would she return? Or would she decide he and his son weren't worth the trouble?

Brayden squirmed in his arms as he carried him

to the family room, and when Luke put him down, Brayden headed straight for his toys. Watching his son play, Luke was relieved that the little guy had finally calmed down. All he wanted was for his son to have a life without turmoil. And now he might have done something that created exactly that.

In the kitchen, there was little evidence that Brayden had eaten supper, but Luke didn't doubt Hayley had made sure he did. After heating the plate of leftovers he found, he was soon settled at the counter, wondering how to apologize to her when she returned from her class. Before he could think of words that wouldn't make him look like a bigger fool than he already was, Brayden came to stand beside the tall stool where he sat.

Luke moved his empty plate aside and pulled his son onto his lap. "You look tired, buddy. Want to go to bed?"

Brayden shook his head, but closed his eyes and snuggled against Luke's chest. Within minutes, he'd fallen asleep, and Luke took him up to his room, where he undressed him and tucked him into bed, hoping that nothing would change by the time Brayden awakened in the morning. They needed Hayley, and Luke silently vowed to do whatever it took to keep her at the ranch for Brayden.

He was putting Brayden's toys away in the family room, when his phone rang. Pulling it from his pocket, he held his breath, hoping it wasn't Hayley calling to tell him that she'd decided not to return. He was relieved to see the number was his sister's, instead.

"So how's Hayley working out?" Erin asked when he answered.

The last thing Luke wanted her to know was that things weren't going smoothly because of him, so he tried for a calm, normal voice and hoped she wouldn't notice anything was wrong. "Just fine," he answered. "Brayden is crazy about her, and she's amazing with him. You were right."

"I won't say I told you so, but I told you so."

Luke's laughter came freely. It was just like his sister, the oldest of the three of them, to make him forget his troubles. When their parents died, she'd been the strong one and kept the three of them together. But as soon as he'd turned eighteen, Erin had been on the road, looking for answers she didn't even know the questions to. He often wondered if she'd found either.

She kept busy with rodeo, so they didn't talk often. Even her visits were brief—when she visited—before she hit the road again.

"She's pretty, too, isn't she?"

The tone in Erin's voice dared him to argue, but Luke didn't rise to the bait. "Very pretty."

"So you like her."

Luke shook his head and chuckled to himself. It hadn't been a question, but a statement. "We both like her. And before you ask, she's at her evening class."

"Well, I just called to see how everything is going. I'm glad it's all good. How about Dylan? Is he doing okay?"

Luke wasn't sure if he should mention how much his brother was struggling. Dylan probably wouldn't appreciate it if Erin learned what was really happening. But since he didn't have a clue what his older brother might do next, there wasn't much their sister could do to help.

"Yeah, he's okay. We had some rain yesterday, but we managed to get caught up on the work today."

"Send some of that rain down here to New Mexico, will you? The ground is as hard as a rock."

"I would if I could."

They talked for a few minutes about the weather and ranching, and then ended the call with a promise to talk again soon. He'd just checked his watch when he heard Hayley's car, and hoped she'd found a way to forgive him for the trouble he'd caused.

Because he didn't want her to think he'd been waiting for her return, he switched on the television, grabbed the newspaper and settled on the sofa. When he heard the door from the garage open, he reminded himself that he still needed to apologize for the entire episode. But he didn't need to grovel to do it.

"How's Brayden?" Hayley asked when she walked into the family room.

Luke saw her worried frown as she stood looking intently at him. "He's okay," he answered.

"You're sure?"

"Yeah, I am." But he was getting the feeling that she was trying to decide whether to believe him or not. "I put him to bed, and last time I checked, he was sound asleep."

Her chin dipped in the slightest of nods. "All right, then."

When she moved to walk away without saying more, he realized he wasn't ready to let her leave it at that. He knew he was a good father. He'd done everything to be the best he could be. Maybe she didn't understand that. "I've spent the past two years with my son, every day, every night. I know if he's okay or not."

She was halfway to her room, but stopped and turned back to look at him. "I never said you didn't."

"But—"

"I only wanted to make sure you weren't saying it because he *should* be all right, not that he was." She shook her head and sighed. "Maybe it doesn't matter."

A pinch of panic made him uncomfortable, but he wasn't going to back away from this. "Yeah, it does, and we both know it. Things have been…strained these past few days. It's been—" But he didn't know if they should be talking about what had happened or if they should simply let it go.

"You're right," she said, surprising him. "It's like we've been walking on eggshells, tiptoeing—"

"That's it, exactly." The relief he felt encouraged him to do what needed to be done and that he hadn't done well earlier. "About the other night in your room…"

She shook her head. "We all do things we shouldn't. As far as I'm concerned, it never happened."

He nodded, not sure if that was good or not. But it wasn't the time to dwell on it. "I'm sorry I forgot about your class tonight and I hope you didn't have any problems because of it. I swear it won't happen again. I'll do whatever I have to do to keep from being late on nights you have class."

There. He'd said it, and he felt better for it. But she didn't seem as pleased by it as he'd expected.

"Promises are easy to make but harder to keep."

"Yeah, I know but—"

"And it's not as if I don't think you'll try to keep your word, but on the other hand, I think this is more important to me than you realize. So here's what I think we should agree on."

He opened his mouth to argue, but instead, he asked, "What's that?"

"We won't have to revisit this topic again, and I'll agree to stay, but with one stipulation."

"What's that?" he asked, although he wasn't sure he really wanted to know.

Her chest rose and fell when she took a deep breath before answering. "I can't be late again. My education and my future are too important to me. And I know you wouldn't do it on purpose, but to keep that from happening, I'm asking for two weeks of severance pay, if it should."

It wasn't at all what he'd expected, but he couldn't think of any reason why he shouldn't go along with her demand. "Okay. Yeah, I can agree with that."

Relief was written in her eyes, and she blew out a breath. "Good. Thank you."

He watched as she turned and continued to her room, hoping he'd never have to test the stipulation he'd just agreed to. Maybe he'd been depending on her too much, but with the ranching situation as unstable as it had been, thanks to Dylan, there wasn't anything else he could do. At least for the time being.

He had to at least admit that he enjoyed her company. She hadn't been working for him long enough, but that didn't change the fact that he couldn't deal with losing her now. And that meant staying on his toes and being the kind of employer she deserved. He just hoped he could do that.

HAYLEY KEPT AN EYE ON Brayden for signs of even the slightest trauma the next morning, but the little guy seemed to be in good spirits. Not only was he in a happy mood, but he offered no resistance when she put him down for a short, morning nap. As a reward, and because she felt a little guilty for upsetting him the evening before, she was busy working on a surprise outing, when he appeared in the kitchen, rubbing his eyes and yawning after finishing his nap.

"Perfect timing!" She placed him in his seat at the counter and moved the sandwiches she was making out of his reach. Brayden refused to eat bread crust, and she'd decided the first day she'd attempted to coerce him into trying that it wasn't worth the struggle. He'd grow out of it, she told herself, although one of her grown brothers still tried to ditch the crust whenever he could. And their mother continued to ignore it.

Handing Brayden a cup of juice she had ready and waiting, she watched as he drank it all, without a break or a breath. "Thirsty, huh?" she asked, refilling the cup and setting it in front of him. "Brayden, what do you say?"

His eyes widened as he looked at her, but he said nothing. Although he could be quite vocal when he wanted something, he still needed to work on his manners and vocabulary. He understood most of what he heard—evidenced by his reaction the evening before to her argument with his father. But his own speech wasn't high on his list. She suspected it was because Luke didn't spend as much time talking with him as a mother might have. Because of that, she made sure she talked to him about everything.

"I have a surprise for you," she said, smiling.

"S'pize?"

At the counter, she put a thermos with juice for Brayden and a water bottle for herself in a plastic tote. "Yes! It's such a nice day, I think we should go to the park. Would you like that?"

"Pawk!"

"You bet! A trip to the park."

"Go pawk!" he shouted, squirming and bouncing in his seat, until she unbuckled the safety strap restraining him and helped him jump down to the floor. "Wuv pawk!"

She laughed, and bent down to give him a hug. "I know you do. So let's get our jackets, and I'll leave your daddy a note so he knows where we are."

Brayden took off with a shout, and she heard his footsteps as he pounded up the stairs. Smiling to herself, she grabbed a pen and paper and scribbled a note for Luke.

After the evening before, she wasn't quite ready to spend a lot of time around him. She'd lucked out that morning, when he'd left before she'd even opened her eyes. Hopefully she'd feel more at ease as the day wore on.

She'd just propped the note on the counter, where Luke would be sure to see it if he came home, when Brayden raced into the room, carrying not only his own jacket, but hers, as well. She thanked him and helped him get his on right side up, then they gathered their things and went to her car.

Hayley filled the trip into Desperation with silly songs and rhymes, and was pleased when Brayden tentatively tried to join in. She'd recognized his shyness the first time she'd seen him, more than likely the result of spending most of his time with his father and uncle. For that reason, and the fact that she didn't intend to be his nanny for more than a few short months, she hoped Luke would soon get Brayden into day care. The little boy needed to be around others—especially other children—to work on his social skills. One more reason she'd decided to take him to the park, hoping there would be other children there.

She wasn't disappointed.

"Hayley, hello!"

As she waved to the young redheaded woman who greeted her, Hayley closed the car door and took Brayden's hand. "Look at the two boys over there," she said to him, recognizing Kate McPherson and her twin sons from the café. "Do you want to go play with them?"

But Brayden's grip tightened on her hand, and he took a half step back. Before she had a chance to encourage him, Kate called to him. "Hey, Brayden, you remember Tyler and Travis. You see them in the Chick-a-Lick all the time."

Brayden nodded, but didn't let go of Hayley's hand. "Let's go say hello to them," she suggested.

He didn't seem to mind when they walked to where Kate stood watching her boys dodge in and out of the elaborate and colorful playground equipment.

"It's so nice to see you again," Kate said, making room on the bench for Hayley. "The twins get tired of each other, so it's great that Brayden is here and they have someone new to play with."

Hayley looked at Brayden, who stood watching the boys play, but didn't make a move to join them. "I think he's feeling a little shy today."

Kate nodded. "It's natural, I hear, but the twins have never been shy. Sometimes they keep to themselves, but I guess that's expected, or so I've heard."

"How old are they?"

"A little younger than Brayden," Kate answered, offering Brayden an encouraging smile. "They won't be two until July."

Hayley nodded. "Luke mentioned that Brayden turned two last month."

"He's done a good job raising him on his own," Kate said, as Brayden started inching his way toward the twins. "It couldn't be easy. Even as much as Dusty adores Tyler and Travis, I don't think he could handle raising even one of them on his own, much less both of them."

Hayley nodded in agreement. "From what I've seen, Luke really tries and is fairly successful. I don't think it's been easy. It's hard enough to raise a two-year-old, but trying to run a ranch at the same time is more than most anyone could do. I have to admit I admire him." And she did. She'd known far too many men who were so wrapped up in their own lives that they weren't always aware of what was going on in their children's. Luke, she was certain, would never be that kind of father.

"I'm just happy that Luke found you to help with Brayden," Kate said. "It isn't easy to find someone in a small town who cares and has the time to do what you're doing. Or even half of what you're doing."

With Brayden now playing happily alongside the other two boys, Hayley could relax. "I'm lucky to have the job."

"And I hope you stay on for a long time."

Just as Hayley started to explain that she wouldn't be Brayden's nanny for more than a few months, a car pulled into the parking area and stopped.

"Oh, good, she finally made it," Kate said, standing. She turned to Hayley. "Have you met my sister Trish?"

Hayley watched as a blonde got out of the car and helped a small girl, who looked about the same age as the twins, from the backseat. "No, I haven't. I really haven't been into town very much, so you and a couple of others in the café are really the only people I've met."

"We'll have to fix that," Kate said with a smile that promised friendship. "Trish, come meet Brayden Walker's nanny. Remember I told you we met Saturday at the Chick-a-Lick?"

Trish waved as she leaned down to say something to the little girl, then straightened and walked toward the bench, where Kate introduced the two.

"I'm sorry," Trish said, with a smile at Hayley. "I didn't mean to appear rude." She looked at Kate and sighed. "I had to remind her again that we don't eat sand. Honestly, I don't know what's wrong with her."

"Maybe she needs more roughage in her diet," Kate suggested with a giggle.

Trish gave her a sisterly punch, and then settled on

the end of the bench. "I asked Paige about it, but she said not to worry. It's just something that some kids do. She'll grow out of it. I just wish she'd grow out of it today!"

Kate, in the middle, patted her hand. "She's perfectly normal in every other way, so stop worrying so much. Aunt Aggie said you used to eat dirt, so it must run in the family."

Trish shot her a look that could kill, followed by her own giggle. Leaning around her sister, she smiled again at Hayley. "Don't mind us. We've always been like this."

Hayley laughed. "I have four younger brothers, so I understand."

"Your poor mother!" Kate exclaimed, causing them all to laugh.

"She loved it," Hayley admitted. "Still does. She seems to thrive on chaos."

"Then it's no wonder you have a talent for children, what with four younger siblings." Kate nudged her sister. "I wonder if either of us could manage that."

"I doubt it," Trish answered quickly. "Especially if they were all sand eaters."

They all began laughing again, and Hayley watched the four children play, marveling at how they'd overcome their initial shyness and were now enjoying themselves. Out of the corner of her eye, she noticed an elderly man hurrying through the park not far away, checking back over his shoulder frequently, as if someone was following him.

"Looks like Vern's on the run again," Kate announced.

Hayley looked at her. “On the run?”

Nodding, Kate chuckled. “Keep watching.”

Within seconds, Hayley noticed a woman, who appeared to be about the same age as the man, hurrying behind him, the purse she carried on her bent arm swaying and knocking against her hip. “Who are they?”

“That’s Vern Isley in the lead.”

“And Esther Watson closing in from behind,” Trish added.

Hayley looked from one sister to the other. “But what’s she doing? Is he trying to get away from her?”

“From what our aunt has told us, Vern and Esther were sweethearts when they were young. Then Vern went off to war, and when he came back…”

“What?”

Kate shrugged as Trish leaned forward to answer. “Nobody really knows. All we can figure is that something must have happened during the time he was gone. Aunt Aggie said his mama died while he was fighting in the war, and maybe that has something to do with it. Most people speculate that Esther just never wanted to give him up, so she keeps trying to catch him.”

“Literally,” Kate finished.

Hayley couldn’t imagine what it must be like for Esther to continue to be that determined, or even for Vern to keep running away from a woman he may have once loved. “But they must be in their eighties.”

“Vern fought in the Korean War, so yes, they both are,” Kate replied. The three of them fell quiet, watching the elderly pair disappear from sight. “I need to be getting home. Are you leaving, Trish?”

"In a few minutes. I promised Krista I'd push her in the little swing. What about you, Hayley?"

"We should be getting home, too. I meant to ask you, Trish. How old is your little girl?"

"Not quite two."

Hayley glanced at the twins. "Then the three cousins are about the same age?"

"Exactly the same age," Kate said. "Trish delivered on time, and I went into labor early. I blame *her* for that."

Trish laughed and wrinkled her nose. "And I'm so proud of doing that for you."

As the two women exchanged sisterly verbal jabs and then laughed, Hayley marveled at them. "How wonderful that the two of you could share that!"

"It is," Kate admitted, "but I really hope it doesn't happen again."

Trish shook her head. "We've decided not to be in a rush, but Morgan would really like to have a son."

"Most men do," Hayley agreed. "And women adore their little girls."

"So do the dads. Or least Morgan does, in spite of being convinced that Krista was going to be a boy."

Laughing, they all agreed and admitted that little boys were just as special to their moms. Kate announced she hoped Hayley would join them soon for another playdate, and Trish echoed the invitation.

After Kate bid them goodbye and left with her boys, Trish spent time with her daughter, while Hayley and Brayden enjoyed a little more time on the play equipment. Hayley felt a warm glow when she saw Brayden's eyes shining with the joy of a little boy who'd spent time playing with friends, and she hoped to remember to get in touch with Kate about a playdate.

Her contentment continued after arriving back at the ranch, and she was able to do some studying while Brayden napped. By the time he was up and going again, it was later than usual, and the two of them waited, not too patiently, for Luke to finish his workday and join them. As the evening grew later, she had no choice but to put a very sleepy and grumpy boy to bed, without a good-night from his father. She wasn't too worried that Luke hadn't spent time with his son. He wasn't the kind of man who would put his family anything but first. But she did fear that this pattern of late evenings could continue. As much as she cared for Brayden and enjoyed her job, she'd worked hard and long to get the education needed to fulfill her dream and, she couldn't let either of those things delay the final step to getting her degree.

"I KNOW. IT WAS LATE last night when Dylan and I finished our work," Luke began, hoping to ease any damage he'd done. "And I know you're thinking it's going to be a habit, but it isn't."

Hayley turned from the sink where she was rinsing breakfast dishes. "I'm not upset, and I believe you. But I think Brayden missed seeing you."

Raking his hand through his hair, Luke tried not to let the frustration he felt get the best of him. "I missed spending time with him, too." He turned to see his son playing happily with his toys at the other end of the room, and he smiled. He hadn't wanted to work late, but Dylan had been manic about getting all the work done. Luke's only choice was to help and hope it wasn't a sign of something else going on with his brother—something that probably wouldn't make life easier for any of them.

"At least it wasn't a night you had class," he pointed out.

Hayley's smile contained a patience he didn't have. "That's true."

He was relieved that she didn't point out that it wasn't proof of anything, and that his promise to not be late again wasn't completely within his power. Not that he was going to allow anything or anyone to make him break it.

"In fact," he continued, "if you have something you want to do—studying, shopping in town, or anything else—I'm taking the morning off to spend with Brayden."

Hayley, who had been loading the dishwasher, straightened and looked at him, her surprise obvious by her wide-open eyes. "That's great, Luke. It really is. And I do have some studying to do before class tonight, so I really appreciate this extra time for myself."

He mentally patted himself on the back for a job well-done, by killing two birds with one stone. Not only was he going to get to spend the morning with his son, but he was giving Hayley some extra time for her studies. What more could he ask for on a Friday morning?

When she'd gone, Luke joined Brayden on the floor. It had become clear that his son's favorite toys had become the ones Hayley had brought for him that first day. He wasn't surprised. They were all well-made and sturdy, with details that were almost real.

Luke was enjoying himself and his son, when there was a rapping sound on the sliding glass doors. They both looked up to see Dylan open the door and step just inside.

"Do you have some time?" he asked.

Luke glanced at Brayden, who was scrambling to his feet. "Better put those cows into the back of the truck, buddy. While you do that, Uncle Dylan and I are going to step outside, okay? You'll be able to see us out there." He pointed to the glass doors leading to the deck.

Brayden hesitated, but returned to his spot on the floor. Luke stood and followed his brother outside, making sure he could keep an eye on his son. After giving Hayley the morning off, he couldn't exactly ask her to stop whatever she was doing to keep an eye on Brayden.

"What's up?" he asked, when Dylan had closed the patio door and the two were outside.

Dylan lowered his head and toed the wood deck with his boot. "I don't want to do this again, but..."

Tension and anger hit Luke like a sledgehammer. He should've seen it coming. Dylan had been working like a madman, but even before that, Luke had seen the signs. Each year as the anniversary of the accident that had claimed the lives of their parents drew near, it was as if Dylan crawled into himself. And each year he took off for a few days to a couple of weeks. This year had been worse than usual, and he shouldn't have been surprised. Dylan's first getaway had been far too short.

"You're leaving again."

Dylan slowly looked up and nodded. "I have to. I

know it makes more work for you, but I'll find someone to help."

"Someone we'll have to pay," Luke pointed out.

"There's money enough for it, at least for a while."

Luke knew it wouldn't do any good to try to stop Dylan, and he would just have to hope that his brother wouldn't be gone long. "If you're sure it will help you, I won't stand in your way. When are you leaving?"

"After the weekend."

"How long do you plan to be gone?"

"When I can get past all this."

Luke nodded, as an emptiness, coupled with apprehension, filled him. Dylan was a good man, but he suspected that depression had a grip on him. All he could do was hope that his brother could find a way to deal with the past. Dylan was far more important to him than having extra work to do at the ranch. "I'll take care of everything," he assured his brother.

"Thanks."

When Dylan started to walk away, Luke reached out and pulled him into a brotherly hug. "Take care of yourself, and if you need anything, you call me."

"I will."

Luke watched his brother leave. He suspected it would be a long while before Dylan could let go of the past. If he ever did. All Luke could do, each time Dylan left, was hope the time away would help his brother. If there was anything else he could do for him, he would. As it was, the responsibility of the ranch was now on his shoulders. There'd be extra work, for sure, even if he hired someone to help while Dylan was gone. Would it be possible for him to keep his promise to Hayley? He didn't know. And if he couldn't, would she have any other choice than to leave?

Chapter Six

Taking a break from her studies, Hayley stepped into the family room to discover Brayden playing quietly in the corner. But Luke was nowhere in sight. "Where's your daddy?" she asked Brayden.

Busy with his toys, he looked up and in the direction of the doors that led out to the deck, then returned to his play.

Although she didn't think Luke would leave his son alone, she still checked to see that he hadn't gone far as she passed the glass doors on her way to the kitchen. To her satisfaction, she saw him on the deck, in what appeared to be a deep conversation with his brother.

In the kitchen, she filled a glass with tea and grabbed a handful of snacks. She glanced toward the deck again on her way back to her room and saw Luke, standing alone as his brother walked away. Brayden still played quietly with his toys, so she returned to her room to study, until she needed to stop to fix lunch.

But as she reviewed one of the procedures she was certain would be on a test that night, she couldn't keep out the vision of Luke, his back to her and his hair disheveled, as he stood on the deck, watching his brother walk across the backyard.

She'd grown up on a small farm, but it hadn't been anything near the size of the operation Luke and his brother owned. Like most farmers and ranchers, both men worked long hours when weather, breakdowns, sick livestock and dozens of other things could change a rancher's schedule in the blink of an eye. Those things not only affected the rancher, but everyone.

She'd known all this and still accepted the job, believing that as long as each of them were aware of the other's priorities, everything would be fine. And then Luke had been late, and she'd been upset. Looking back on it, she regretted issuing the ultimatum. It would be difficult for him to stick to it, although she was certain he would try.

She forced her attention back to her studies, but in the back of her mind, she hoped either she or Luke would come up with some kind of backup plan, just in case. At least now he seemed to have an idea of how important her education was to her.

She broke away from studying again and discovered a note from Luke saying he'd taken Brayden into town, and that they'd be back late that afternoon. Glad for even more time with no interruptions, she returned to her room.

When a knock on her door broke her concentration, she glanced at her watch and realized it was much later than she thought. Pushing away from the desk, she closed the thick anatomy book. Having Luke in her room again wasn't a good idea, in spite of his attempt at apologizing, and she scrambled to find the shoes she'd kicked off earlier.

"Just a minute," she called, as she discovered them under her bed.

"It's getting kind of late," Luke said from the other side of the door. "Isn't it almost time for you to leave?"

"Yes, it is." She slipped on the shoes and hurried to open the door. "I guess I lost track of time."

He stepped back, giving her plenty of space to step out of the room and close the door behind her. "I hate to bother you," he said, "but I thought you might be late if I didn't."

His concern made her smile, and when she looked up at him, she noticed again how good-looking he was. "Thank you, Luke. I appreciate it. Really."

He shrugged, as if embarrassed by her thanks, and moved away.

She followed him to the kitchen, where Brayden sat in his seat, his eyes bright when he looked up at her.

"Did you have fun with your daddy today?" she asked, taking a seat at the counter.

"Fun," he said, and then looked at Luke. "Da-dee."

"He's talking more, now that you're here," Luke said.

"And doing a good job of it," she agreed, laughing. Glancing at Brayden, she noticed his cheeks were pink with what she guessed was excitement, and she wondered if he might be a little tired. "Did he take a nap?"

Luke settled at the end of the counter. "Two. A short one this morning before we went into Desperation for lunch, then he slept all the way home from Edmond."

She listened to Brayden's sometimes nonsensical jabber and watched how he interacted with his dad. They'd both obviously enjoyed spending the day together.

Standing, Luke put his hand on Brayden's shoulder. "Until these last few days, I never realized how much I missed spending time with him."

"I'm glad you enjoyed it," she replied, looking from one to the other. "Maybe you can do it more often."

"We're going to try, aren't we, buddy?" he asked his son. He turned to Hayley. "It's getting late. You might want to get on the road."

A quick look at her watch, and Hayley jumped to her feet. "You're right. I need to change and get going."

But Brayden shouted, "No go!"

"It's okay, buddy," Luke said, as Hayley hurried to her room. "She'll be back later. Remember?"

As she hurried to change her clothes to something more appropriate for her class, she could hear that Brayden wasn't at all willing to let her go or tell her good-night, but there wasn't time to calm him before leaving. As it was, she was going to have to hurry if she wanted to make her class. And this time it was her own fault, not Luke's.

Grabbing her books and purse, she hurried out of her room and found Luke trying to interest Brayden in his toys. It was plain to see it wasn't working, as Brayden tossed one toy after another across the room.

Even though she was in a rush, Hayley stopped to give Brayden a hug. But instead of calming him, as she hoped it might, he howled his displeasure that she was leaving and attached himself to her legs.

"Brayden, honey, I'll be back," she assured him. "I'll be here when you wake up in the morning, just like always."

But Brayden didn't give up the stranglehold he had

on her legs, even when she tickled his most ticklish spot where his neck met his shoulder. "No go!"

"Maybe I can get him to let go," Luke said, reaching for his son.

"No, let me talk to him. If that doesn't work..." She paused with a shrug. She wished she had more time, but if she didn't get out the door soon, she'd be late, and two times could be disastrous.

Tossing her books and bag aside, she managed to lower herself to one knee. Obviously sensing that she couldn't skip out on him while she was kneeling, Brayden loosened his grip. Hayley scooped him into her arms and held him.

"You've had such a fun day with your daddy," she said, keeping her voice low, "and I know you don't want me to go. Sometimes you don't like it when your daddy leaves, either, right?"

With a tearful sniff, Brayden nodded.

"He always comes back, doesn't he?" He nodded again, and she hurried to make her point. "I need to leave to go to school, but I'll be back before you wake up in the morning, and we'll plan something extra fun to do."

"How about our Saturday trip to the Chick-a-Lick?" Luke suggested. When Brayden nodded again, Luke glanced at Hayley. "If you don't mind," he added.

Hayley managed to straighten, and with Brayden's grip loosened, Luke was able to ease him away from her. "I can't wait to go to the Chick-a-Lick with you tomorrow!" She grabbed her books and bag, then walked backward toward the doorway. But when she turned for the door, she could hear Brayden's wails behind her. Her heart broke, but she couldn't stop.

Once she was in her car and on her way, she convinced herself not to worry and that Brayden was doing fine. She was just entering the outskirts of Oklahoma City when she realized he'd felt a bit warmer than usual. Of course, he'd spent the day with his dad, something he didn't get to do as much as he had in the past, so she had to take that into consideration. But as she drove on into the city, she remembered how bright his eyes and pink his cheeks had been at supper, and she wondered if he might have a temperature.

Waiting until she reached the parking lot of the building where her class was held, she reached into her purse for her cell phone to call Luke. But her phone was missing. Frustrated and running late, she did a quick search of the interior of her car, but came up empty-handed. There was nothing she could do. As soon as class was over and she was back at the ranch, she would check on Brayden. Until then, all she could do was hope Luke would notice and do whatever was needed.

"WHY DID I EVER THINK raising a kid would be easy?"

Luke, on his hands and knees and with sponge in hand, mopped up what looked like a gallon or two of water on the floor of the upstairs bathroom. He not only had a mess to clean up, but he'd had an evening he hoped he'd soon forget.

The second that Hayley was out the door and on her way to class, Brayden had thrown the mother of all tantrums. After realizing that shouting at his son didn't do any good, not even to get the child's attention, Luke tried everything he could think of to get him to calm down. In the end, Brayden had given in to exhaustion. And then came bath time.

As he mopped up the mess, Luke thought back to the days immediately following Brayden's birth. Kendra had changed over the course of her pregnancy, from a misty-eyed bride to a woman Luke had barely recognized. Between the weight gain and the morning sickness, all she seemed to talk about was how much she looked forward to her baby's birth—when she could get back to normal again. Luke had chalked it up to pregnancy hormones. He'd been wrong. By the time Brayden was six months old, Kendra had left and filed for divorce, giving him sole custody of their son.

His attitude toward his ex-wife had changed, and he tried not to let his son see it. He knew Brayden had missed the mothering that babies needed, and he continued to try to fill in for that, although it hadn't been easy.

Brayden had taken to Hayley almost instantly, and for that Luke was grateful. But in the back of his mind he feared the inevitable. One day, maybe soon, Hayley would leave, and not just to attend a class, but forever. He didn't want to think what that would do to his son.

Or to him.

Shaking the worrisome thought from his mind, he stood and surveyed the floor. It was still damp, but there wasn't a puddle in sight and it would soon be completely dry. A quick glance at his watch told him that Brayden had been quiet for at least fifteen minutes and had probably fallen asleep. Still, checking on him would be a good idea.

He'd just stepped out of the bathroom when his cell phone vibrated in his back pocket. Pulling it out, he saw that his sister was the caller. Surprised, he pushed the talk button.

"Hey, Erin."

"Can you tell me what's up with Dylan? He called a few minutes ago to ask about my schedule. When has my schedule ever been of interest to him?"

Luke wasn't sure exactly how to answer. "What did he say?"

Erin let out an obviously frustrated sigh. "He just wanted to know about my schedule. I told you."

"Maybe he's taken an interest in your riding?"

"Sure," she answered, her voice filled with sarcasm. "It's a little late for that, don't you think? Now what's going on?"

Luke knew he didn't have a choice. "He's having a rough time."

"About what?"

He hesitated. Erin had never been able to accept their brother's yearly escapes, and he suspected she had been more affected by their parents' deaths than she let on. "You know. It probably has something to do with the accident. Spring is coming on and—"

"It's been fifteen years," she said, as if that would be the end of the subject.

He suddenly realized that she knew exactly how long it had been. It would have taken a quick calculation for him to come up with exactly how long ago their parents had died, but his brother and his sister were both fully aware of the exact length of time.

"He's taking some time off," he admitted.

"Again? How long this time?"

"I don't know, but my guess would be a substantial amount."

After a short silence, she asked, "Do you think he wanted to know my schedule so he could catch up with me? Is that it?"

"I don't know, Erin, but would it be such a bad thing if he did?"

This time the silence lasted a little longer. "No, I suppose it wouldn't. But how are you going to handle all the ranch work?"

He moved to lean back against the wall and switched the phone to his other ear, giving him time to form the best answer. "I'll hire some help if I need to."

"Seems like a waste, but I guess if he needs time off, it's the only thing to do. I still don't see why he needs to talk to me, though."

"I guess he'll tell you when he's ready."

"Yeah, maybe. When is he leaving?"

Seeing no other way out than to tell her everything he knew, he quickly gave her a rundown of what Dylan had told him. "That's all I know."

With little more to say, Erin said goodbye, and Luke heaved a sigh of relief. He pocketed his phone and walked into the semidarkness of Brayden's room. The small night-light cast shadows against the wall as he adjusted his sleeping son's blankets. Leaning down to kiss his forehead, his lips touched hot skin.

Brayden was sick. And if the heat radiating from the little guy was any indication, he was burning with fever.

Hurrying to the bathroom where he hoped he could

find a thermometer, Luke felt his heart pound. Shortly after Kendra had left, Brayden had gotten sick. His fever had shot up and he'd suffered a seizure. Doc Priller, who was still practicing at the time, had told Luke that at Brayden's age, it wasn't unheard of. All he knew now was that if his son had a fever, it was serious, and his hands fumbled as he searched through the medicine cabinet.

Finally finding the thermometer, he pulled it from its case and pushed the button to turn it on. Nothing happened. Of all the times for the battery to be dead, why did it have to be when there was an emergency?

Sprinting down the stairs, he hoped there might be a spare in the downstairs bathroom, but all he found there were Hayley's things, tucked away in the medicine cabinet, out of sight.

Before panic set in, he gained control. There was fever reducing medicine upstairs. He'd seen it while looking for the thermometer. Even if he didn't know how high Brayden's temperature was, he could still get started on bringing it down, before he called the doctor.

He'd almost reached the top of the stairs when he heard a sound and then Hayley calling to him. He groaned with the feeling of relief. At least he wouldn't have to worry alone.

"HE'S DEFINITELY A sick little guy," Hayley whispered, leaning over Brayden, whose cheeks were bright pink from the fever. "Did you take his temperature?"

"The battery in the thermometer must be dead. It wouldn't turn on."

She moved to reach for the bag she'd grabbed from

her room and pulled a thermometer from it. “This checks the tympanic membrane temperature,” she explained, “and is a lot quicker than others.”

“Is it accurate?”

She placed the tip in Brayden’s ear. “If used correctly.” Seconds later, it beeped, and she removed it and checked the reading. It was much higher than she’d suspected. “It isn’t good,” she said, looking up at Luke, whose face was pinched with worry.

“How high?”

“One hundred three point seven.” She watched as he turned to leave. “Where are you going?”

“I was on my way to get the fever reducer when you came in.”

“Bring a cool, but not cold, damp cloth, too. Maybe I can start bringing down the fever before the medicine kicks in.”

While Luke retrieved the needed items, Hayley removed the blankets that were covering Brayden, and then unbuttoned the pajama top he wore. She didn’t want him to get a chill, yet she knew it wasn’t good to keep him bundled up, either.

As she tried to make the little boy as comfortable as possible, Luke returned and handed her a bottle of acetaminophen and a plastic syringe made for administering liquids to infants. “I’ll warn you. He isn’t going to like this,” Luke said.

“He doesn’t get a choice,” she answered. “Now prop him up a little bit so I can give him this without it choking him.”

Luke did as she instructed, and she easily had the

medicine in him without even a protest. "He really is sick," Luke said, his voice filled with concern.

"Sick enough that he doesn't know much of what's going on," she agreed. "Does he get sick often?"

"No. Not since he was six months old, when pretty much the same thing happened."

Alarmed, she glanced up at him and immediately saw how worried he was. She looked at the little boy lying next to her on the bed, his thick, dark lashes resting on cheeks that were far too pink. "Tell me what happened the last time."

"His fever shot up and he had a convulsion."

Exactly what she'd feared. "A febrile seizure?"

"Yeah, something like that."

She pulled her stethoscope from her bag and placed the chest piece on Brayden, listening. She thought she heard rales or a crackling sound in his lungs, but couldn't be sure.

"Why do you have that?" he asked, indicating the stethoscope draped around her neck.

"To check his lungs and make sure this isn't because of some respiratory bug."

He shook his head. "No, that's not what I meant. Why do *you* have one?"

"Oh! Well, because I'm a registered nurse and—"

"You are?"

"Why, yes. Didn't I tell you that?"

"I guess I knew you were going to some kind of medical classes, but I didn't know what kind."

"I've already earned my nursing degree. Now I'm studying to be a PA."

"Right. A physician's assistant. You mentioned

that. I guess I didn't know or understand all that." He glanced down before looking directly at her. "I'm sorry I've made it harder for you."

He sat on the edge of the bed, watching his son, and she nearly placed her hand on his shoulder to reassure him, but stopped herself. Getting too close to him, whether emotionally or physically wasn't a good idea. Not now or at any time.

Worry creased Luke's face. "What else can we do?"

She placed the damp cloth on Brayden's chest. "I'll check his temperature again in a few minutes to see if it's starting to go down. If he's responding to the acetaminophen, we can relax a little."

"What if he doesn't?"

The last thing she wanted to do was give him more to worry about, but she felt she couldn't keep anything from him. While she was pretty certain that what she suspected was moderate dehydration, and a high fever wasn't life threatening, the previous seizure meant there was really only one thing to do. "You need to call the doctor, Luke."

Chapter Seven

Luke stood, nodding. "I was going to do that when I heard you come in. I'll have to get the number from downstairs." His stomach tightened in a knot. Images of the night Brayden had had the seizure came rushing back, and he couldn't shake them. He'd let down his guard and forgotten that time. *Until now.*

He was pretty much convinced Hayley knew what she was doing. Even he knew Brayden was inching toward danger. He should've seen it earlier. Brayden hadn't been nearly as active as usual. He'd been happy to play with his toys and had definitely not wanted Hayley to leave for her class. A good father would have known. He still had a lot to learn.

Grabbing the cordless phone in the kitchen with one hand, he pulled the list of emergency numbers from the drawer beneath it, then punched in Tucker O'Brien's number.

It was late, but not too late, and Tucker answered. "Hey, Luke, what can I do for you?"

"Is Paige there?" Luke answered, starting up the stairs. "Brayden's sick."

"Hang on," Tucker said. "She's right here."

Within seconds, Luke heard Paige's voice. "What's going on with Brayden, Luke?"

"Sorry to call you so late," he said, trying to keep the worry from his voice. He explained about Brayden's past seizure, current temperature and how they'd given him something to bring it down, but that it hadn't, at least so far. "Since Hayley is a nurse, she knew what to do, but she also said I should call you."

"A nurse? I wasn't aware of that," Paige answered. "It sounds like it might be a good idea if I have a look at him. Bring him in right away. I'll meet you at the clinic. Just park behind the building and come to the back door."

Having reached Brayden's room, where Hayley stood watching and listening, he nodded. "Okay. We'll be right there. And thanks." He turned to Hayley. "We're to take him in now."

Hayley nodded. "Wrap him loosely in the blanket, so he doesn't catch a chill, while I get my shoes and a jacket."

She left the room, and he turned to look at his son. Why hadn't he noticed that his son wasn't feeling well? Instead, he'd just been glad Brayden hadn't demanded a lot of his attention, especially when Dylan had given him the news that he would soon be leaving again.

It sure hadn't been a good day, he thought, as he carried Brayden down the stairs. He found Hayley in the kitchen, refilling the juice cup.

"Ready?" she asked, coming around the counter, cup in one hand as she struggled with putting on her jacket.

He immediately moved to help her, noticing how dark her eyes were. She was as worried as he was.

Following her out to the garage, he thought about how calm she'd been, how she'd taken over so easily the moment she walked in from her class. He hadn't realized until now how really competent she was, especially in a crisis.

"Let's take my car," she said. "You can drive."

Nodding, he settled his son in the backseat of her car. It took some adjusting to make the harness fit around Brayden and the blanket, but Luke finally had his son secured in the child safety seat. Brayden immediately began to whimper.

"I'll sit in the back with him," Hayley said, handing Luke her car keys.

He took them and climbed in behind the wheel, while she slipped into the back with Brayden. Inserting the key into the ignition, he realized his hands were shaking. Why not? His son was sick, very sick, and he was taking him to see the doctor in the middle of the night. What parent wouldn't be worried?

"It's okay, Brayden," Hayley said from the back of the car.

Luke glanced in the rearview mirror. "We're going to visit your favorite doctor. I bet you'll get a sucker and everything."

"A sucker!" Hayley exclaimed, obviously trying to distract Brayden, who continued to whimper.

He could hear Hayley's soothing voice, calming Brayden, and it wasn't long before it was quiet in the car. Quiet enough that he could worry again.

"What do you think it is?" he asked her.

"It could be anything. More than likely, some kind of virus."

"Then they can give him some medicine or something."

"For the symptoms, yes. But if it's a virus, those usually have to run their course," she explained. "Hopefully, if this is a virus, it's easy to treat."

His hands tightened on the steering wheel. "If I'd been watching him, I would've noticed that—"

"Don't blame yourself," she said, silencing him. "Kids get sick. Besides, it isn't any more your fault than mine. There's no telling where he might have picked up something."

"If anything happens—"

"Luke." Her voice held a warning. "This probably isn't as serious as you seem to think it is."

"But the high fever and dehydration—"

"Aren't all that uncommon. But that doesn't mean we should ignore the symptoms. We need to deal with them first. Taking him to see a doctor is the best thing we can do for him. If this is something other than a virus, the doctor can give him something. If it is a virus, at least you'll be assured that he's being taken care of by a professional."

"But you're a nurse," he pointed out.

"I'm also very close to him. Even doctors get another opinion when it comes to family. Stop worrying. We're doing the right thing."

Nodding in the darkness, he hoped she was right. He didn't know what he'd do if anything happened to his son.

LUKE PARKED THE CAR behind the one-story, brick building of the local doctor's office and carried Brayden to the door, where a single, protected lightbulb shone over the heavy metal door. While they waited for the doctor to open the building for them, Hayley tucked the blanket tighter around the little boy. The air held more of a chill than she'd anticipated, and she didn't want to expose him to the cool, night air.

She heard the sound of the doorknob turning and stepped back to stay out of the way. But Luke moved aside. "Go on in," he said, as the door swung open.

Smiling at the woman who held open the door, she walked into the building, and then waited while Luke entered with Brayden. They followed the woman down the dim hallway and into a small but brightly lit examining room. Hayley blinked at the light as she moved to an out-of-the-way spot and watched Luke try to settle a very unhappy Brayden on the examining table.

His face drawn and worried, Luke spoke over his shoulder to the woman. "Paige, this is Hayley Brooks, Brayden's nanny."

"I'm Dr. O'Brien," she said, offering her hand to Hayley, who took it. "Kate and Trish mentioned they'd met you. Welcome to Desperation. I wish we weren't meeting under these circumstances."

Hayley thanked her as the doctor turned to wash her hands in the tiny sink. She was surprised she hadn't known until that moment that the doctor was a woman. Not that it mattered.

"It's all right, Brayden," the doctor said, drying her hands. "We're going to help you feel better." After picking up an otoscope and tongue depressor from the top of a small, metal cabinet, she turned back to Luke. "Tell me what's been going on."

He glanced at Hayley, before answering. "Well, to be honest, I didn't really notice he was sick. He was grumpy earlier, but we had a full day. I thought he was tired and sent him to bed. I didn't realize he was sick until a few minutes before Hayley came home from her class. I was getting ready to call you then."

When the doctor turned to her for answers, Hayley didn't have many answers. "I wasn't with him much," she admitted. "Luke—Mr. Walker—gave me the day off, so I spent most of it in my room, studying. The one time I stepped out for a few minutes, Brayden was playing quietly with his toys. It wasn't until later in the evening, when I was leaving for class that I had much contact with him."

"He wasn't rubbing his ear or anything?" the doctor asked, checking Brayden's ears and throat.

"Not that I noticed."

"Tummy ache?"

"He didn't appear to have one."

"Luke?" the doctor said. "Did you notice anything?"

"Not at the time. But now that I think about it, he was quiet. All day. Just played by himself, mostly. We went into Edmond and picked up a pizza, but he didn't seem sick, just quiet." He ducked his head before continuing. "Dylan and I have been pretty busy, so he's spent most of his time with Hayley. It wasn't until Hayley started to leave this evening that Brayden… Well, he had a tantrum."

"He was clingy," Hayley explained, "and he felt warmer than usual, but I thought it was because he was upset. You know? I was running late and didn't think too much of it, until I was pulling into the parking lot for class at OU."

"I had a devil of a time giving him a bath," Luke continued, "but I finally got him into bed. It was maybe twenty minutes or so later when I went in to check on him. That was when I noticed he was hot. Real hot."

All the while they were describing the events of the day, the doctor was doing a thorough examination. "When did you take his temperature?" she asked.

"Hayley did. When she got back from her class, she went to check on him. I should have noticed sooner that something was wrong, but—"

"It's not your fault," Hayley replied, not wanting him to take the blame for something that couldn't be blamed on anyone. "I missed it earlier, too."

"We're lucky," he told the doctor. "She's studying to be a doctor's assistant. I figured she knew what she was doing."

"A doctor's assistant?" The doctor turned to Hayley. "As in a PA?"

"I hope to finish my masters this spring and graduate."

"And you're working, too?"

Hayley nodded and smiled, knowing what was going through the doctor's mind. "I know, it's frowned upon, especially during these last few months, but I took a long, hard look at what working and finishing my degree would involve, and I feel I can do it without endangering my education."

The tiny lines between the doctor's eyes deepened, but she didn't try to argue or point out the hazards. Instead, she turned back to listen to Brayden's chest with her stethoscope. Hayley could tell she wasn't convinced, but she already knew those hazards well.

Even knowing them, she'd had two reasons for taking the job her aunt's friend had suggested. First, she needed money to help defray her student loans and also to pay for a place to live. And second, she'd believed that being the nanny for a two-year-old boy wouldn't keep her from her studies. The first wasn't debatable, the second was, and she'd been right. The job wasn't a problem. It was her growing feelings for and attraction to her boss that were proving to be trouble.

"What was Brayden's temperature when you took it?" the doctor asked, while taking it again.

"One hundred three point seven," Hayley quickly answered. "That was about ten-thirty, and I gave him the recommended dose of acetaminophen. Then we removed his blankets, hoping that would help cool him."

"You didn't sponge him?"

"A little, and we tried to get him to drink some apple juice. He barely sipped it."

Dr. O'Brien checked her watch. "His temperature should be down by now, but it isn't."

"That's why I called you," Luke said.

"I'm glad you did. Fevers aren't abnormal. They're an indication of illness, of the body fighting an infection or virus. But when they get too high, especially in children, there are times they can result in convulsions. That's why we're especially watchful and try to keep fevers down as much as possible. And because Brayden has experienced a febrile seizure in the past, he's at risk for another."

"I guess I'm lucky Hayley knows what she's doing," Luke admitted.

Hayley felt her face grow warm. "I'm glad I could help."

"Did you notice anything else, Hayley?" Dr. O'Brien asked.

Hayley glanced at Luke before answering. "I thought he might be a little dehydrated, so with the fever not responding to the acetaminophen, and the history of seizure, I thought a doctor should see him. I also listened to his chest and suspected there might be a problem, so I told Luke to call you."

The doctor nodded. "I heard the same. It was wise to insist he bring Brayden in tonight." She moved to the sink to wash her hands again. "Luke," she said over her shoulder, "would you help Brayden button his pajama top?" When she finished, she settled on a metal stool and looked up at Hayley. "I don't know if you might be interested, but there's a strong possibility that we'll be expanding the clinic in the very near future. Maybe even more, depending on what the county and state have to say. I'm sure we'll have some openings, if, after you finish school, you want to join us."

Hayley smiled at the doctor's offer, pleased at her thoughtfulness. "That's very nice of you, but I haven't decided yet what I'll do after graduation. I've had an offer in Oklahoma City, although I haven't accepted it. But I'll certainly keep you and Desperation in mind."

Her attention was immediately claimed by Brayden's loud protests, as Luke attempted to keep him distracted, and she moved to help. But her thoughts were on the doctor's offer. The one she'd spoken of in Oklahoma

City wasn't official, but she held out hope that it was. Two of the doctors there had been integral in her dad's recovery from the stroke he'd suffered shortly after she'd taken a break from college to plan the wedding that never happened. It had been one of those doctors who'd mentioned that she might look into becoming a PA. Staying in Desperation had never been part of her plan. Once graduation was over, she wanted to find a position in the city. By then, she hoped a spot would open for Brayden in one of the two day care facilities in Desperation.

Calming words whispered to Brayden quickly began to soothe him, and she focused her attention on what the doctor was saying to Luke. She'd suspected they wouldn't be going directly home, and the doctor's instructions to Luke proved her right.

"To be safe, I'd like him to go to the hospital for a short stay," Paige told Luke. "If all goes well, I don't expect him to be there for more than a day or two. There's some congestion in his chest that could be a sign of pneumonia. It may be nothing, but I'd rather be safe than sorry."

Not a fan of hospitals, he frowned. "There's no chance Hayley could take care of him at home?"

"Luke," Hayley said, still holding Brayden's hand, "he'll be much better off and get well much faster if he's where he can be given everything he needs. And to be honest, I wouldn't feel comfortable caring for him at home, no matter what."

Paige pressed a hand to his arm. "It's the best thing for him. And for you. This way the dehydration can be watched and taken care of, and he'll be treated for anything else, should there be a need."

"All right," he conceded. "If you both think that's the best thing."

When Paige gave instructions to take Brayden to a hospital in Oklahoma City, Luke questioned the decision. "Why not the county hospital over at—"

"I'm afraid not," Paige answered with a shake of her head, while writing in what Luke guessed was Brayden's chart. "I had word today that they're at half staff there, due to funding cuts. That should change soon, but for now they're shorthanded."

He had no choice but to give in. "Okay. Whatever you say. You're the doctor."

Paige smiled before going back to the paper. "Let me finish this, and then I'll call and let the hospital know you're coming."

"Will you be coming, too?"

"I can if you think I need to."

Again, he looked to Hayley, who shrugged one shoulder. "I'm sure he'll do fine with the staff there," she told him. "I know some of the nurses and have no doubt he'll get great care."

Stuffing his hands in the pockets of his blue jeans, he waited. He'd never given much thought to what might happen if Brayden got sick. He guessed he'd put that one time out of his mind and expected his son to be as healthy as *he* was.

And now he was getting ready to take his little guy to the hospital. But if Paige said it was the right thing to do and Hayley agreed, then that's what he'd do.

Paige closed the folder she'd been writing in and

picked it up. "If you'll all wait right here for a few minutes, I'll go call the hospital and let them know you're coming."

Luke nodded, but said nothing and checked his watch. At some point, he'd need to call Dylan and let him know what was going on. There was no telling how long Brayden might have to stay in the hospital, so his brother might just have to delay his plans to leave, at least for a while.

"I hate to admit it," he said, "but I'm worried."

"Anyone would be in your situation," Hayley replied. "But I don't think there's reason to be overly concerned. Brayden's normally a healthy little boy."

"That's exactly what worries me."

"And worrying never solved anything."

Luke immediately stiffened, but although Hayley's words had scolded, the concern on her face was proof that she hadn't been trying to brush off his feelings. She understood. And she was right. He could worry until the cows came home, as the old saying went, but it wouldn't make Brayden any better.

"You're right," he said. "He'll get the care he needs and be home in no time, healthy and happy."

Her smile was soft and understanding. "Brayden will be fine."

"Yeah, he will."

The door opened and Paige walked in. "The hospital is expecting him, so you can be on your way. I've given them instructions, and I'll stop in to see him tomorrow, unless you'd rather I checked on him tonight."

He looked at Hayley, who gave another noncommittal shrug. She wasn't going to help him with this.

He didn't like any of it, but he did believe they knew what they were doing. Maybe it was time to trust them.

"You're sure he's not in any danger?" he asked.

"Only if we ignore the symptoms," Paige answered, "And we aren't doing that. He'll be in good hands, Luke—I promise."

Admitting to himself that he'd probably been luckier than a lot of other parents, he nodded. Things had been pretty easy with Brayden. "I know that. So what do we do when we get there?"

"Take him in through the emergency room entrance. They'll check him over before taking him to a room in pediatrics."

"I'm familiar with the pediatrics unit," Hayley told Luke, "and it's great."

"I have no doubt he'll get excellent care," Paige assured him. "They know where to reach me if needed, although I doubt that will happen."

"Then let's get going," Luke said, picking up his sleeping son from the examining table.

"Take an extra blanket," Paige said, reaching into a drawer beneath the exam table. Handing it to Luke, she put her hand on his shoulder. "Drive safely and stay within the speed limit. If this was an emergency, I'd call the fire station and have them send the ambulance. Okay?"

"I promise to keep us all safe."

Paige followed them out to the car and waved as they drove away. In the backseat, Brayden was snuggled in his car seat, sound asleep. As Luke pulled out into the street, he turned to Hayley. "Here's hoping they get him well, fast."

Chapter Eight

While Luke filled out the necessary paperwork at the main desk, Hayley waited with Brayden in the examining room of the hospital's emergency center. She had no qualms about the care from the nurses. She knew and had worked with several of them, including the one who was taking Brayden's vitals and charting them.

"Poor baby," the nurse crooned. "We'll get you well real soon, sweetie."

Before Hayley could ask about his temperature, another nurse she knew from nursing school stepped into the room to stand beside her.

"Hayley, how do you keep from just gobbling him up?"

"He *is* a little sweetheart," she answered. "But—"

Tammy leaned closer. "Not to mention that his daddy isn't hard on the eyes. Don't tell me things haven't been…well, interesting."

Hayley had worked enough with Tammy in the past to know that she was famous for starting rumors with simple innuendos that could quickly grow to epic proportions. She needed to stop even the slightest hint of gossip immediately. "I'm Brayden's nanny, Tammy," she answered. "His father is my boss and I'm his employee. That's it. Nothing more."

"Then you're not nearly the woman I thought you were when we were in school."

Hayley had had enough. "That's unprofessional of you to say, and you know it. That little boy over there," she said, pointing to Brayden, "is very sick, so unless you're here to assist Shirley with vitals and charting, please leave."

Tammy opened her mouth as if to argue, but then shrugged and left the room, without another word. Hayley could only hope she'd nipped any talk in the bud, but she wasn't counting on it.

"Good for you," the nurse looking over Brayden said.

Hayley turned and tried for a smile. "Thanks, Shirley, but it probably didn't do much good."

Shrugging, Shirley jotted notes on the chart, then set it aside and turned to Hayley. "She's a good nurse. One of the best. But she needs to take some lessons in how to keep her mouth shut and her nose out of other people's business."

Hayley couldn't have agreed more, but was saved from saying so when Luke walked in.

"How's he doing?" he asked her.

She looked at the other nurse. "Shirley?"

"All I can tell you is that his temp is still elevated. The doctor should be here any minute, and I'm sure he'll—"

As if on cue, the door opened and a tall, smiling man walked in. "I heard you were here, Hayley."

Surprised to see her favorite doctor, she flashed him

a bright smile. "I see you're still determined to become a doctor."

He laughed and extended a hand to Luke. "Dr. Derek Hunt. Hayley and I worked together for several months."

Luke glanced at Hayley as he took the offered hand. "Luke Walker. Brayden—the patient—is my son."

"I'm Brayden's nanny," Hayley explained.

"And I'll bet you're good at it," he replied. "So let's take a look at this little guy."

After a thorough exam and a dozen questions asked and answered, he stepped back. "The chart says he was referred by a Dr. O'Brien in… Desperation?"

Luke, standing near by, cleared his throat. "Dr. Paige O'Brien."

"I'm not familiar with the name or the town."

"About an hour drive from here."

He nodded again and put the chart aside, looking past Luke and directly at Hayley. "What drew you to a small town? From what I remember, you'd vowed never to live near one again."

She looked at Luke, and then back again at Derek. "I'm working there at Luke—at Mr. Walker's ranch, caring for Brayden."

"So you've given up on your plan to become a PA?"

"Not at all," she announced, glancing again at Luke, who appeared to be engrossed in the conversation. "I hope to be finishing my masters this spring, and then I'll be looking for the right place to work."

Derek leaned back against the examining table, while he made notes in the patient chart. "I'm glad to hear it. I always said you had what it takes."

Embarrassed by the praise, Hayley answered with a smile. "Thank you. I appreciate your faith in me, Derek." When Brayden began to fuss, she moved to pick him up. "I'm assuming you're going to admit him," she said, glancing at Brayden in her arms.

"Of course." He straightened and put the chart aside. "We'll do a blood test, after we get him to his room, but I suspect this is bacterial. We'll put him on an IV to ward off any more dehydration and to administer antibiotics, if it is bacterial, and keep him here a day or so, depending on how he does." He turned to Luke, who stood silent and solemn by the door. "Once we know he's in the clear and on the mend, he can go home."

"Thanks," Luke replied.

Derek started for the door, but stopped as he reached for the handle. "I'll have a nurse take you up to pediatrics. It's great seeing you again, Hayley. Maybe we can grab a cup of coffee the next time you're in the area."

"That would be nice."

When the doctor was gone, Luke walked across the room and took a fussing Brayden from her. "You and the doctor obviously know each other real well," he said, after trying to calm his son.

"Everybody knows everybody in a hospital," she said with a shrug. "It's like a small town. Or maybe even a family. I can honestly say that Dr. Hunt is one of the best doctors here, not to mention a nice person. And I'm not the only one who thinks so."

Luke nodded, but didn't look directly at her. "He seems to know what he's doing."

The conversation was interrupted by a young, auburn-haired nurse, who held the door open for the orderly with a gurney. "Is this Brayden?" she asked. Luke assured her that it was and that he was Brayden's father. "We'll take him up to his room now," she said.

Brayden took one look at the rolling bed and let out a scream that would curdle cream. Luke tried to calm him down with, "Look at the neat bed," but Brayden was having none of it. Even Hayley couldn't stop what bordered on hysteria.

After sending the orderly and the gurney on their way, the nurse turned with a smile. "Don't worry about it. It happens. Sometimes little ones just don't like it. We do have an alternative, though."

Luke looked at Hayley before asking, "What's that?"

"If you'd like to get into the wheelchair, you can hold him on your lap."

"I'll let Hayley ride in the chair with him," Luke said.

Knowing she wouldn't be allowed to go up to the floor with them, Hayley quickly shook her head. "No, Luke. It would be better if you take him."

With a shrug, he took a seat in the chair, and Hayley settled Brayden on his lap. The little boy's terror quickly subsided to quiet sobs, as he buried his face in Luke's chest.

"We'll have him tucked into bed and feeling better in no time," the nurse assured him.

"I see there have been some updates made to the building," Hayley said, as they stepped into the hall.

"A few since you worked here," the nurse answered, then gave Hayley a sheepish smile. "Oh, I'm sorry, but I know who you are. I'd just started nursing school when you were accepted into the PA program. There was quite a lot of excitement among the nurses who knew you."

Hayley wasn't sure if that was good or bad. Either way, she wasn't someone who liked being in the limelight, so she changed the subject as they moved down the hallway. "What's the patient load like right now?"

"Because of cuts, we're shorthanded, but there aren't as many patients as we had a couple of months ago."

Hayley nodded. "It ebbs and flows."

"Do you miss it?"

It wasn't a question Hayley thought about often, so it took her by surprise. "Sometimes," she admitted, "but I think I'm going to enjoy working *with* doctors, instead of *for* them."

The nurse laughed, and then hurried ahead of them to push the elevator button. "I'm Amy," she said when they reached her. "There's a recliner in the room, Mr. Walker, if you plan to stay the night. And blankets in the closet behind the door, if you need them."

Hayley felt Luke watching her, and she suspected she knew why.

"We'll both be staying," he said.

Hayley started to answer, but Amy spoke first. "I'm sorry, Mr. Walker, but Miss Brooks can't stay."

"What do you mean, she can't stay?

"She isn't a family member."

"Well, that's damn crazy," he announced from his position in the wheelchair. "She's a nurse, and I'll feel better if she's here with my son."

"She'll be able to visit tomorrow during visiting hours."

"That doesn't make sense."

Hayley decided it was time to intervene. "Luke, she's a nurse," she explained. "It isn't her job to make the rules, only enforce them."

His eyes narrowed. "I didn't know you wouldn't be allowed to stay, but I guess you did."

"Yes, I knew."

"And you didn't tell me."

She felt as frustrated as he obviously did. "I never really gave it any thought. He'll be fine," she reminded him. "What's important is that you'll be there. I'll be back in the morning, and you can always call me if you have questions."

Her words didn't seem to ease his concern, but he nodded. "Where are you going to go? It's late, and I don't think you should drive back to the ranch alone."

When the elevator door opened, Amy held it for them. Hayley smiled at his concern. "It's only an hour drive. I'll be fine."

"All right," he said, "but be careful."

"I will. Now get Brayden up to his room, and I'll see you tomorrow."

He nodded, then reached for her hand and held it, thumb caressing the tops of her fingers. "Thank you, Hayley."

Far too aware of his touch, she eased her hand from his. "You'd better get going."

"Yeah." He glanced up at the nurse and nodded. "Yeah, we'd better get going."

Amy backed the chair into the elevator. Just as the doors began to close, Hayley saw Luke's tired smile, and he waved. Returning the wave, she sighed, feeling as if she'd run a marathon. If the pounding of her heart had been the only indication, she might have.

Outside in the cool night air, she looked up at the sky, studded with stars. It was going to be a long night.

LUKE SPENT A RESTLESS night next to Brayden's hospital bed in a recliner that was a twin to the one that had belonged to his dad. Even now, his dad's recliner still had a place in the house where he and his brother and sister had grown up. He decided that memories may have had something to do with his fitful dreams that had included bits and pieces of his childhood and the parents he'd lost fifteen years earlier.

At some point during the predawn hours, he heard a nurse say softly that Brayden's fever had broken and his temperature was slowly going down. Luke wasn't sure if he'd said anything to her or not, but when he awakened a few hours later to his son's constant demands to see "Haywee," he knew the little guy was on the mend. And he couldn't remember when he'd ever felt so relieved.

Hayley arrived after Brayden had finished his breakfast, and she seemed as relieved as Luke felt. "I doubt we could have done what they've done here at the hospital to turn him around so quickly," she said when she heard the news.

"He's on antibiotics for what they've decided was a touch of bronchitis," Luke explained. "They said he's already beginning to respond to those, too."

Hayley leaned down and gave Brayden a long hug. "I missed you," she told him, "and I'm so glad you're better this morning!"

"Go," he answered, his lower lip pushed out and a deep frown on his face. "Wanna go."

"Not yet, buddy," Luke told him, looking at Hayley. "If he takes his meds without giving them any trouble, they said he'd have a better chance of going home soon."

She nodded. "It does make a difference, and I know he'll be good," she said, before turning to Brayden. "Won't you?"

"No!"

Luke and Hayley both laughed. "Oh, he'll take them, all right," Luke said. "I don't want to spend many more nights in that torture thing they call a chair."

"Recliners are nice for short naps, but they weren't made for all-nighters."

"I'd be crazy to argue," he answered, reaching around to his back and faking a groan. When she laughed, he felt better...about his back and everything, and laughed with her. "You're amazing," he said, then wished he could take it back when he saw the crimson on her cheeks.

She walked to the window, before she spoke again. "Did they give you any indication of when he might get to come home, other than soon?"

"When his temperature is normal and the antibiotics have kicked in."

"That's good news."

He couldn't have agreed more. He'd talked to Dylan earlier and explained that he wouldn't be around to do chores for a couple of days. When he'd explained why, his brother had voiced his concern that Brayden was going to be okay. He'd assured Dylan that the trip to the hospital might have made the difference between a sick little boy and a very sick one. He had Hayley to thank for that. She'd remained calm when he'd nearly lost his cool. While he'd known what to do, she'd been the one who had made sure that he followed through and did it. And he needed to let her know how much he appreciated her and everything she did. He just wasn't sure how to do that.

By the next day, Brayden was released, with instructions to see Dr. O'Brien in a week for a quick checkup to make sure everything was all right. As Luke watched Hayley help Brayden dress for the trip home, he noticed how quickly his son seemed to tire. The fever and infection had taken a toll on the boy, causing him to lose his usually sunny disposition. Hayley wasn't going to have an easy time of it, until Brayden was back to normal, and Luke wondered what he could do to make things easier for her, in the meantime.

The trip back to the ranch was at first a little noisy, with Brayden voicing his complaints from the backseat. Even though he was getting better, he wasn't one hundred percent and would have to take it easy for a few days.

Once they were home and Brayden was settled in his bed, surrounded by his favorite toys and with an array of healthy snacks and a drink at his side, the first thing he did was fall asleep. His long eyelashes nearly hid the dark circles under his eyes that Luke hoped would soon be gone. Until they were, he wouldn't rest easy about his son's health.

As if she could read his mind, Hayley said, "He's

out of danger, Luke. He'll be back to normal by the end of the week."

"Yeah, I suppose he will," he answered. At the moment and except for those barely noticeable circles, Brayden looked rested and healthy. But he wasn't. Even a few days was too long to wait to see him bouncing around the house again or have him hanging on his legs. Luke missed both already.

Downstairs again, he took a seat at the counter. "It'll be an early night for me, that's for sure."

"I hope it won't be a late night for me, either." Reaching into the refrigerator, she produced two glasses of tea.

"Why would it be?"

Placing his glass within his reach, she took a seat at the end of the counter and tipped her head to the side, a quizzical expression on her face. "Why, because it's Monday."

"Monday?"

"I have a class." She glanced at her watch. "In fact, I'm going to have to hurry if I want to get out of here on time."

His first thought was to ask if she could stay. He wasn't feeling secure about taking care of a sick boy on his own, but he quickly realized that, after all she'd done for Brayden and him over the past few days, he had no right to ask more of her.

"I should've remembered," he answered. "Is there anything special I need to do while you're gone?"

Shrugging, she shook her head. "Brayden should be fine. I found a baby monitor in an upper cabinet. We can set it up so you can hear him from down here.

When I get back from class, I'll put the receiver in my room, so you won't have to get up in the middle of the night."

He wasn't completely comfortable with the idea. "But you'll have to be running up and down those stairs," he pointed out. "You know, there's an extra bedroom up there. It's right next to Brayden's room and practically empty. I can move your bed up there while you're at your class."

"That's too much trouble," she said, with a shake of her head.

"No, it isn't. And I'll feel better with you closer to him."

"But—"

"Look at it this way," he said, before she could argue, "I won't have to worry about you falling down the stairs in the middle of the night. Another trip to the hospital isn't on my list of something I want to do again for a long while."

"Well…"

The way she dragged out the word, he knew she was tempted. He was sure it wouldn't take much to convince her. "Those stairs can be treacherous in the dark, especially if you're not completely awake."

"There's the lamp in the upstairs foyer. And the night-light near the stairs down here, too."

He suspected he was losing. "But—"

"I've checked on him before at night, so it's okay. There's no need for you to go to any trouble." She stood and picked up her glass. "I'd better get going or I'll be late. I should be back in time to give Brayden his next dose of medicine, so you don't have to worry about that, but he could wake up and need help with something to drink."

Knowing that arguing with her wouldn't help and with time slipping away before she needed to be on the road, he kept his opinion to himself.

"I have my cell phone," she said, fifteen minutes later, when she was walking to the door to leave. "I'll keep it on silent, in case there's an emergency, and I'll call you during break to check on how you're both doing."

"We'll be fine."

She was about to step out the door when she turned to him with a smile. "I'm sure you will be. Try to get some rest, okay?"

Before he could answer, she was out the door and halfway to her car, so there was no sense in mentioning that moving the bed wasn't a big deal. He wanted to do something to make everything easier for her. She obviously wasn't going to let him, and he wasn't sure what he could do about that. Or even if he should try. It didn't take much to know that his problem was caring too much. And that was trouble, all the way around.

BY THE TIME HAYLEY returned from her class, it was later than she'd planned and past time for Brayden to have his medication. The house was quiet and Luke was nowhere to be seen, so she guessed he'd gone on to bed, as she'd hoped he would. She'd missed Brayden while he was in the hospital, and unfortunately she'd found herself missing his dad, too. That wasn't something she should be doing, and she needed to remedy that as soon as possible. Once she had her degree, she hoped to find an opening in Oklahoma City. Luke would have to find someone to take care of Brayden, but wasn't that what the plan had been all along? She'd never considered being a nanny for any longer than she needed to. She was too close to her dream to let anything—even an adorable two-year-old boy and his daddy—keep her from getting it.

Upstairs in Brayden's bedroom, she did a quick temperature check. He woke just enough to take the dose of medicine, and then fell instantly back to sleep. Once she was assured he was all right, exhaustion hit her like a sledgehammer, and it was all she could do to go downstairs to her room, slip into her nightgown and slide under the covers. As her eyelids grew heavier, she made a quick check that the baby monitor was on next to her bed, and then finally gave in and fell asleep.

It seemed as if only minutes had passed when she was awakened by the sound of Brayden crying and calling for her. Still half-asleep, she hurried up the stairs, only to realize halfway there that the usual soft glow of the lamp was missing, and it was pitch-black. Carefully and slowly, she somehow made her way in the dark to Brayden's bedroom.

"It's all right," she crooned as she stepped into the room, where at least a bit of light from his night-light cut through what would have been complete darkness. Making her way to his bed, she eased down on the side of it and reached for the thermometer she'd left on the small, bedside table.

He was warm to the touch, but not hot, and she guessed his fever still remained within normal. The thermometer beeped and, with a quick look at it in the light just bright enough to see it, she knew that all was well.

"Would you like some juice?" she asked him, fluffing his pillow behind him, and he scooted up to lean against it.

"Jooze," he answered, his voice raspy with sleep.

She reached for the small thermos she'd left on the table and poured him half a cup of apple juice. "Here you go."

He took it with both hands and drank it all without taking a breath. As she took the cup from him, he struggled to keep his eyes open and finally slipped under the covers again without a request for more.

Hayley sat with him for a while, watching him and listening to the rhythm of his breathing. When she was sure he was fully asleep, she carefully moved from the bed and stepped away.

At the doorway, she wondered again what had happened to the lamp Luke always kept on at night. It had been on earlier, shining her way up and down the stairs. Now, even the night-light in Brayden's room didn't reach beyond his door.

For a moment the dark hallway disoriented her, and she reached out to find something that felt familiar. She knew the stairs were on the left, but she couldn't remember exactly how far. She took a deep, slow breath and remembered that the small table with the lamp was just past the stairway, next to the door that led to Luke's bedroom. If she walked straight ahead, she could reach it and turn on the light. But she had to be careful. If she took a wrong step and veered too far to the left, she might tumble down the stairs, just as Luke had warned.

Seconds ticked by as she took tiny steps, her hands stretched in front of her until she touched what she knew were the double doors of the master bedroom. Letting out the breath she'd been holding, she turned to her left and bumped into the table, where the lamp always sat, nearly knocking it over. Just as she let out a small shriek of alarm, she heard a noise and suddenly felt a solid, warm body collide with hers.

"What the—" came the rough and sleep-laden male voice, as large, strong hands took hold of her.

Heat shot through her like a bolt of lightning. "It's—It's me, Luke. It's Hayley," she managed to say.

"Hayley?" he repeated, sounding as disoriented as she'd felt only minutes before.

His hands moved on her back in what felt like a caress, and her breath caught, silencing a moan of need that shocked her.

"Hayley," he repeated in a whisper, and she felt the touch of his lips in her hair.

"Um, Luke?" she said, alarmed by the sensations racing through her. "Maybe we should turn on a light?"

His hands stopped moving. "A light?"

She knew he was fully awake when he quickly pulled away. Somehow she managed to find her voice and hoped that he couldn't detect the slight wobble in it when she spoke. "The lamp wasn't on when I came up to check Brayden. And I guess I wasn't awake enough to give it much thought. At least not until I was ready to go back to bed and realized I couldn't see where the stairs were. It was foolish of me, I know, but—"

"Very foolish. You could have taken a wrong step and gone right down those stairs."

She felt him move closer again, and his arm brushed against her. She heard the click of a switch, but nothing happened.

"Bulb must have burned out during the night," he said. "Stay right here and don't move. I'll turn on the light in my bedroom and the bathroom light so we can see where we're going."

The bathroom light! Why hadn't she thought of it, instead of trying to feel her way in the dark? But she knew the answer. She hadn't been as awake as she should have been, and she scolded herself for being so irresponsible.

Blinking at the light filling the hallway, she suddenly realized she'd also forgotten to slip on a robe. While her nightshirt wouldn't be considered even close to daring, she felt uncomfortable, especially when his eyes raked over her.

"Thank you. I can make it back to my room now," she told him, hoping he didn't notice her embarrassment. She started down the stairs, wishing she could disappear, but stopped when he spoke again.

"Tomorrow we're moving your things up here."

She turned to look back at him, convinced it would be the worst thing to do. "But—"

"No arguments, Hayley."

From the look on his face, she knew better than to argue.

Chapter Nine

"I must have been crazy," Luke muttered to himself three days later. Things shouldn't have been much different than they were before he'd helped Hayley move to the upstairs bedroom next to Brayden's, but they were. And it was taking a toll on him.

When he finished washing his hands at the sink in the garage, he dried them, and then took a deep, steadying breath, before going into the house and heading for the kitchen. All he wanted was something to drink.

He'd left Dylan's as soon as they'd finished filling the last of the big grain bins. It wouldn't be long until his brother would be leaving, this time for what he guessed would be an extended period. Maybe if he could understand, he could help, but even Dylan hadn't been able to explain, except to say that he had to get away.

Luke filled a tall glass with cold water and drank it quickly. The chill of it made him shiver, and he felt more in control of himself. There was no reason he couldn't walk up those stairs, stop in Brayden's room to say hello, and then go on to his own room to clean up before supper. Not one single reason.

Once he was upstairs, he went directly to Brayden's

room, where he discovered his son, totally enthralled in the book Hayley was reading to him. *Reading.* Something he hadn't thought to do for far too long. Something he should have been doing every night. How had he forgotten?

Just as he began to wonder how he would fit one more thing into his already overscheduled life, he looked up to see Hayley warning him to be quiet with a finger held to her lips. With a nod, he stepped out of the room and into the hallway, relieved that he wouldn't need to stay in the room with her. Since they'd collided in the dark, his already-weakened immunity to her had almost completely disappeared.

Trying to ignore thoughts he shouldn't be thinking, he went to his bedroom, where he showered and changed, hoping he could find something to keep him busy and out of the range of Hayley for the rest of the evening. It wouldn't be completely possible. There was supper to get through, and even if she vanished or he managed to, there was still the knowledge that she was nearby. Very nearby.

Downstairs in the family room, he turned on the television, thinking he might catch the news. Instead, he got caught up in an old rerun of an oddball comedy he'd enjoyed years before. So involved that he didn't notice the room growing darker, he came back to reality with a start when a loud crack of lightning lit the room and thunder shook the house. A split second afterward, the television went dark.

"What the—"

Except for the next flash of lightning, all light had vanished. The house was as dark and silent as a tomb.

It took him a second to get his bearings, and then he hoped the thunder hadn't frightened Brayden. The little guy was out of danger and doing better, but Hayley had mentioned that until he had his energy back, they needed to try to keep him calm and quiet.

Walking in what he hoped was a straight line to the kitchen, Luke was grateful for another flash in the sky to illuminate the room. It was enough to get him to the counter so he could feel his way to the drawer where he knew he would find a flashlight.

Once he had light, he headed for the stairs and bounded up them, afraid to call out for fear that Brayden might miraculously still be asleep. But before he reached the top, he reminded himself of what had happened when he and Hayley had collided in the same hallway, only a few days earlier, and he took the steps slower, checking ahead with the beam of light.

"It's okay," Hayley said from above. "I have some candles."

"Is Brayden upset by the storm?" Luke asked, knowing how his son hated lightning and thunder.

"He's sleeping, thank goodness."

She appeared at the top of the stairs, the candle she held casting a glow over her face. He nearly missed the next step. "That's good," he answered, unable to come up with anything else to say at that moment. "There should be a small flashlight in the drawer by Brayden's bed."

She stepped back, giving him plenty of room as he reached the top of the stairs and stood with her in the hallway. "I have it in my pocket," she answered, "but the batteries must be dead."

Aggravated at what seemed to be a run of bad luck with batteries, he grunted. "There's some in the drawer in the kitchen." Just to be sure he kept on the straight and narrow with her, he took a step back. "Emergency candles in the pantry, too."

"That's right. I'd forgotten I'd seen them there. I'll get mine, too. Maybe there will be enough so we don't run into anything."

Or each other, he thought. When she disappeared into her room, he called after her. "I'll get the candles in the kitchen."

While he retrieved them, he found the number for the electric company and called on his cell phone, hoping to find out how long the blackout might last. But the news wasn't good. One of the main rural stations in the area had been hit by lightning, and it could be as much as three days before power would be restored. He decided not to tell Hayley right away, unless she asked.

Ten minutes later, after she'd finished placing candles around the big room, he excused himself to check on Brayden. Finding his son sleeping soundly, he stood for several minutes, watching him. He'd never dreamed he'd be raising a child on his own. If anyone had suggested that he might, he would've laughed. Yet here he was, doing just that. It wasn't easy. It never had been. And lately, if it hadn't been for Hayley… But he knew that going there wasn't going to make the evening go any easier on either of them.

"I put another blanket on him," he told Hayley when he returned to the family room, "and grabbed a couple for us. I'll get a fire going, too. It's getting colder."

"What can I do?" she asked.

He wasn't sure what else they might need, but then he remembered one thing. "If you don't mind, take the flashlight and go out to the garage. By that door in the back that leads outside, there's a workbench. There should be a radio on it, and it should have fairly fresh batteries. If not, we'll find some around here somewhere."

Nodding, she hurried out of the room, and he heard the door to the garage open and close. While she was gone, he moved the smaller of the two sofas to face the fireplace, where there were still plenty of logs filling the bin.

By the time she returned from the garage, he was kneeling on the hearth, watching the kindling catch and burn brightly. "It won't be long," he said, then turned toward her.

He'd never denied that she was a beautiful woman, but standing in the candlelight, she looked like an angel. Her head was tilted slightly to the side, and her smile was tentative, almost as if she wasn't sure it was okay to smile. He started to get to his feet, ready to walk over to her, until the crack of a burning log brought him to his senses.

Don't do anything crazy.

Yeah, that was all he needed to do, and Hayley would be gone in a flash. And just where would lusting after his nanny get him? Looking for a new one and trying to console a two-year-old, that's where. It was time to get a grip.

"I turned it on and got some static," she said, leaning down to place the radio on the small table in front of the sofa.

Her hair fell forward, and he stared at the slope of her neck it revealed. "What?" Hearing the coarseness in his voice, he cleared his throat and suddenly understood she was talking about the radio. "Then the batteries must be good," he managed to say with what little common sense he could muster.

"Is there a particular station that's best for the weather?"

He hesitated before stepping up beside her. "Yeah, I'll get it."

As he struggled to tune in the radio station that would have up-to-date information on the storm, he noticed that the lights from the fireplace and the candles they'd managed to find didn't reach out very far. And while each of them going to their respective rooms might have been a good idea, he had a feeling that if they did, he wouldn't get much sleep. In spite of the lack of light, it was still early, and if that or the storm didn't keep him awake, wondering how she was faring in the other bedroom certainly would.

Maybe this would be the best time to prove that the attraction to her that had grown since the first time he'd laid eyes on her was nothing to worry about. As if it was a sign, the radio station he'd been searching for suddenly came in loud and clear.

With a smile of satisfaction, he stepped back and picked up the two blankets he'd brought from upstairs. "There's no telling how long this storm might last. Time to get comfortable."

FOR A MOMENT, HAYLEY thought she'd heard a tone in Luke's voice that she hadn't heard before. She hated to label it, but it sounded suggestive. Even seductive. But when she turned her head just the tiniest but to glance at him, there was no indication that he'd been either. In fact, he appeared to be focused on the voice of the weatherman on the radio.

She let out the tiny breath she'd been holding.

"It's definitely getting rough out there," he said, his attention still on what was being said over the airwaves.

"I hope it doesn't last long," she ventured.

He turned his head to look at her. "There's no way of knowing, at this point. From what they're saying, it could keep this up for the rest of the night."

"But is it supposed to get worse?" Having been born in Oklahoma and lived there all her life, Hayley understood the weather and how conditions could change quickly. It was one of the drawbacks of living in the middle of the country.

"They aren't saying."

"But what are the possibilities?" she asked, growing impatient. "Have they mentioned them?"

"No particulars."

She couldn't believe it, so she reached out to turn up the volume on the radio. She had no intention of sitting around all night, while he did or didn't give her the information she wanted and needed.

He turned to look at her, one eyebrow lifted, and it was hard to read what he was thinking. If turning up the volume bothered him, she didn't care, and he might as well get used to it.

"So you're one of those people who likes to know what's going on."

For some reason she couldn't explain, his comment surprised her. "Yes, I am," she admitted.

"But it's impossible to control the weather."

"Of course, but that doesn't mean that I don't want to know what's going on. If I need to take some kind of action, I want to know so I can. I may not be able to control the weather or a lot of other things, but I can control how I react to certain things."

She didn't even notice that he'd taken a step closer, until she looked up and saw the flecks of gold in his blue-gray eyes. Her breath caught in her throat and she couldn't move. Her mind suddenly filled with the memory of the kiss they'd shared.

"What kind of things?" he asked, his voice rough as it seemed to move over and around her.

Opening her mouth to answer, she didn't seem to be able to form a thought, much less the words she knew she needed to say. His smile was slow, warming her from her toes to the pit of her stomach, as fingers of heat skipped over every inch of her, until she thought she couldn't stand it another second if he didn't touch her.

Just as she felt her betraying body lean toward him, he moved back slightly and put a folded blanket between them. For a moment, she still couldn't move, then she forced herself to take the blanket and even managed what she hoped was a smile. "Thanks," she said, but her voice didn't sound like her own, and she wished she'd just been quiet. A simple nod of thanks would have sufficed.

"Which end do you want?"

Her mind still wasn't ready to catch up and work like it should. "End?"

He'd moved away and answered over his shoulder. "Of the sofa."

"Oh, of course," she stammered, feeling like a fool and hoping he didn't notice. None of what she'd thought had just happened had probably taken place. She was acting like a schoolgirl. "I'll take that one," she answered, pointing to the end on her left. "It's closer to the stairs."

"Sounds good." He moved the radio to the center of the table, and then turned to her with a mischievous grin but didn't say anything else.

Still feeling shaky, she quickly took possession of her corner of the sofa and curled up in the blanket. Once he settled at the opposite end, she felt halfway safe and almost sane.

Neither of them spoke for several minutes as they listened to reports of the weather. Hayley wondered if she should go upstairs and check on Brayden, but she couldn't seem to make herself move. A quick look at her watch told her it hadn't been that long since Luke had gone upstairs to check on him, so she was certain he was probably all right. Knowing Brayden as well as she now did, she felt certain that if he awakened, he'd let them know, loud and clear. He was getting better, and therefore grumpier and more vocal.

"So tell me about Dr. Hunt."

The sound of Luke's voice startled her, but his question surprised her even more. "There's nothing to tell."

"Yeah? He seemed to take quite an interest in you and talked like he knew you well. Very well."

It was the way he said "very well" that alerted her. Was he jealous? He couldn't be. She was imagining things. Or was she?

"I take your silence for a yes," he teased.

"Not at all," she countered. "We worked together in the hospital for a short period. Like many doctors and nurses, we formed a professional respect for each other. Nothing more."

"Pretty much what I guessed," Luke said, laughing. "I just thought there might have been some history there and was curious."

"Nothing of interest," she said, hopefully putting the subject to rest. Derek Hunt had been kind to her when she'd been feeling sorry for herself because of Nathan. Needing to change the subject, she asked if the storm was going to cause more work for him and his brother.

"A little. Mud makes things less possible."

It was her turn to laugh. "You and Dylan have done a lot on your own."

"I guess we have. A few people didn't think we could do it, but most everyone helped us in one way or another. All we had to do was ask, and even when we didn't there was always someone lending a hand or giving needed advice."

Hayley thought of the people she'd met since becoming Brayden's nanny. "I've noticed that there's a preponderance of good people around Desperation."

"Most of them. Not all. There are a few in Desperation who were determined to make it hard for us. My guess is that it was because they were hoping to get their hands on the land." His sigh seemed to fill the room, and she waited for him to continue. "We had a dickens of a time at first. If it hadn't been for Erin fighting to keep everything, there's no telling what might have happened."

She understood, completely. "We nearly had the same problem. We've always been a close family, but my dad's stroke brought our family even closer together for some of the same reasons." She had to chuckle at the thought. "I'd hate to be someone who tried to tangle with any of us."

"Do you miss them?" he asked, leaning toward her. "You've obviously been on your own for a while. Do you visit them?"

The touch of yearning in his voice reminded her that she did miss her family. "Not as often as I should," she admitted.

"You talk to them, though, right?"

"I try." But she knew it wasn't as often as it should be, and she quickly made a promise to herself to call her parents soon.

"It's funny," Luke continued, "but I see my brother every day. We talk. Have normal conversations. But we don't really say anything. It's all about things related to the work that needs done and not about us. Even Erin has trouble talking and doesn't call often. It's been almost a year since she's been home to even say hello. Brayden barely knows her."

Hayley's heart broke at the sound of regret in his voice, and without thinking, she moved to put her hand on his. "I wish I could help. If there's anything I can do..."

For a moment he didn't move, and then he turned

his head to look at her. "I've been putting off telling you, but Dylan has decided to leave."

It was almost *déjà vu*. She'd always felt that learning his brother was leaving had been a big reason why he'd hired her. "Again?" She felt bad for saying it and hurried to add, "For how long?"

He shook his head. "He doesn't know. I'm not even sure he'll be coming back. He's never gotten over what happened to our parents. I don't know that he ever will."

"You'll have more work than you can handle."

"I'll hire some help."

All she could think about was how he'd have to take the time to train someone—if he could find anyone to hire. Until school was out for the summer and high school students were cheap, it might not be easy to find help. "That could be costly."

He looked down at her hand, still resting on his, and moved closer, stopping within mere inches of her. With his other hand, he reached up and touched her face. "You're very important to us. You know that, don't you?"

Unable to answer, she nodded. Without meaning to, she curled her fingers around the hand beneath hers. Her mind and body had surrendered to his touch. She would have stopped, if she could have, but she'd lost that power.

He moved even closer, and she closed her eyes, waiting for the inevitable. She felt his fingers trace her cheek, and then his lips, whisper-light beneath her ear, sent mini shock waves through her. *How long has it been?* She sighed, and his lips moved to hers. *Too long.*

His kiss was tentative, as if he were asking if she

was willing. When she responded with some of the passion that had begun to consume her, he deepened the kiss. His hand moved to the back of her head, his fingers diving into her hair. Tipping her face up, he started to move over her, and she leaned back to accommodate him.

Just when she thought she might never be able to stop him, even if she wanted to, he pulled away.

"Maybe I should go check on Brayden," he said, his breathing heavy.

"I can do it," she said, sitting up as he straightened and moved back.

"No, you stay here and stay warm. I'll go." He nodded toward the radio on the table, when he said, "Sounds like the worst is over."

As he walked away into the darkness, she called to him, as if they hadn't just begun one of the best necking sessions she'd been a part of for quite some time. "I'll help in any way I can."

A moment of silence ended with, "I know."

She watched him head in the direction of the stairs and then disappear. Whatever was going on between them, it kept getting stronger. Now that he'd left her to check on Brayden, her common sense took over, and she knew she shouldn't have allowed what had just happened. Earlier that day, she'd given some thought to resigning, but she couldn't quit now, knowing Dylan would soon be leaving, even if she thought it would be best.

"THAT'S THE LAST OF IT." Dylan tossed the duffel bag behind the pickup seat and closed the door. Turning, he squinted into the noontime sun. "It was real nice of Hayley to take Brayden to her parents' home for the day. Gave us more time to get everything done before I leave."

Luke nodded. "Still no idea of where you're headed?"

Dylan looked away, and shook his head. "Not really."

Left with nothing to say, Luke nodded again. He'd have given anything if he could think of a way to help his brother, but instead of helping, he always seemed to say something to make things worse.

"I know this isn't making things easy on you, Luke."

"I've told you before," Luke said quickly, "you don't have to apologize. Just—" He looked out over the outbuildings of the ranch where they'd grown up and felt pride in all the things they'd done over the past fifteen years. Somewhere deep inside, Dylan had to feel it, too. "You really think there are answers out there?"

Shaking his head, Dylan shrugged. "I don't know. But I don't know what else to do."

Luke wished he could understand, but he didn't. "I hope you find whatever it is you need."

"Thanks."

"And don't worry about things here. I can manage."

Dylan met his gaze and smiled. "I know you can. You're the reason I can leave and not worry about the ranch." When Luke started to argue, Dylan put up a hand. "Now don't you think you ought to be leaving? That's a five-hour round trip."

Putting his worries aside, Luke slapped his brother on the shoulder. "You're right. You take care of yourself. And call. Often."

Once in his truck, Luke headed south. He'd dropped

Hayley and Brayden at her parents' farm in the southwest corner of the state the day before. He'd suspected she needed time away from him, and he wasn't sure he could blame her. He hadn't been able to keep away from her and knew it had been wrong to kiss her again. With luck, Brayden hadn't picked up on anything, too excited about going on an overnight trip. He'd chattered and bounced for two hours on the drive there, then fell asleep the last thirty minutes.

After dropping them off at the Brooks farm, Luke had driven on into the Texas panhandle to look at some cattle he'd been thinking of buying. Afterward, he'd returned home to finish what needed to be done before Dylan left.

The return trip to the farm proved to be going quicker than he'd expected. To keep his mind busy and not on Hayley, he started planning how he'd handle the ranch on his own for an extended period of time. It might be a little tough at first, but he had faith in himself that he could do it. Having Hayley there to handle the care of Brayden made a big difference. He needed to find a way to let her know how much he appreciated her and everything she did for them, but he'd probably already managed to botch that, too.

When he pulled into the Brooks's yard, there was no sign of anyone around. But as soon as he parked and stepped out of his truck to walk to the two-story house, the front door flew open and his son burst outside.

Short legs took the steps slowly from the porch to the ground, but once his feet hit the flagstone walk, Brayden raced to grab Luke by the legs. "Daddeeee!" he shouted.

"Hey, there, buddy," Luke said reaching down to pick up his son and give him a hug.

"He's been watching out the window since this morning."

Luke looked up to see Hayley standing on the porch, her arms folded on her chest. He took her all in, from her hair knotted high on her head, to the ragged pair of jeans covered in patches and her bare feet. As his heart rate kicked up a notch, he wondered if he was the only one who reacted to her the way he did. He doubted it. He was pretty sure she'd had more than her share of admirers.

"Dylan and I finished up the last of the work that needed to be done," he explained. "He's probably long gone by now."

Even from several yards away, he could see her frown, as she walked down the steps toward him. "I was hoping he'd decide to stay," she said, followed by a soft sigh.

He switched Brayden to his other arm. "No such luck. But it'll be okay. I can handle it. And if I can't, I'll hire someone to help."

"Did he mention where he's going?"

"He said he doesn't know."

She shook her head. "He really should see about getting some counseling. Whatever this is, it isn't affecting just him."

"I know. It's not like no one has told him that." All Luke could do was hope his brother would finally be able to sort things out on his own, put the past behind him and get on with his life.

"Maybe you should tell him how you feel."

He looked into her eyes and saw true concern. If only he knew what he wanted. Not just from his brother and life in general, but from her. "I wish I knew how."

She nodded and put her hand on his arm, making him even more aware of her and how much his feelings had grown in only a short time.

"I know it isn't easy," she said, lifting her gaze to his, her smile soft and sweet and all for him.

For a moment he forgot where he was, forgot that he held Brayden. It wasn't until the little boy reached his small hand out to touch her cheek that Luke felt the full force of how much he cared about her. If only he felt free to touch her again the way his son did. But he couldn't. He'd learned that the other night. He had to find a way to stop his impulses, before something happened that they'd both regret.

"I'll work on it," he told her, hoping his voice didn't reveal what was going on inside him.

He wasn't sure how long they stood there, but the moment ended at the sound of a voice calling out to them.

"Good to see you again, Luke."

He looked up and past Hayley to see her oldest brother walking down the steps toward them. "A little later than I'd planned," he answered.

"I'm glad it is," Chris said. "I told Brayden he could help us milk the cows."

Hayley turned to grin at her brother before winking at Brayden. "He's been excited all day about it," she told Luke. "I hope you'll stay long enough."

"When we leave is up to you."

She glanced at Chris before speaking. "I was thinking of staying another night."

That was news to Luke, and he didn't know how to take it. He'd dropped them off at the Brooks farm the day before, and now he'd come back to pick them up so they could all return home, just as they'd planned. "But how would you get back to Desperation?"

"Chris has to go to Oklahoma City early tomorrow morning, so he said he'd take me."

Luke looked from her to her brother and hoped his disappointment didn't show. "Whatever you want to do."

Silence fell between all of them, until Chris spoke. "Doesn't matter what you two decide, cows need milked. If you still want to get in on it, Luke, we'd better get moving."

Luke looked at Brayden, still in his arms. "Do you want to help Chris milk the cows?"

Brayden's head bobbed up and down so hard, he would have coldcocked his dad, if Luke hadn't tipped back his head, laughing.

Chris laughed, too. "I guess that's a yes. All right, just follow me, and we'll have you fixed up in no time."

Luke suspected Brayden wouldn't last long, but there was no backing out of it. After a quick look at Hayley, who nodded what he suspected was encouragement, he caught up with Chris.

"Cow!" Brayden shouted.

"You bet, buddy." But even his son's excitement couldn't erase the uneasy feeling he had about Hayley's decision not to go back to Desperation with them.

Was she having second thoughts about continuing as Brayden's nanny? And if that was it, did he have himself to blame?

Chapter Ten

Hayley watched Luke set Brayden on the ground, and then they followed her brother through the door of the barn. More confused than ever, she wondered if she'd made another mistake by choosing to send Luke and Brayden back to the ranch without her. It wasn't that she didn't plan to return, but she needed time away from both of them to sort through the confusion she'd been feeling since before Brayden's trip to the hospital.

With a grunt of disgust at herself, she turned for the house. It wasn't natural for her to be so unsure of herself. She'd always known what she wanted, and she'd always gone after it, whatever it was. But now, she wasn't sure. Nothing seemed like the right thing to do.

Pushing all thoughts of Luke from her mind, she searched for her mother and found her in the kitchen. "Can I help?"

Sharon Brooks's hand stilled on the metal lid of the last of the jelly jars she was unloading from a box. "I was just going to look for you and see if you wanted to take a walk with me."

"A walk?" Hayley could hardly remember a time when her mom wasn't on her feet, moving from one place to another as she cared for a family of seven people.

With a flash of a smile over her shoulder, Sharon placed the jar with the others in the cupboard. "I know what you're thinking. I walk miles every day in this house. Why more? But life has slowed down, what with you and your brothers gone. Your dad usually goes along to keep me company—or at least that's what he says—but he had some bookwork he wanted to finish today."

"Daddy's doing all right, isn't he?" Hayley knew he'd been one of the lucky ones who had not only survived a major stroke, but overcome the effects of it.

Sharon nodded. "As good as new. Or close, anyway. Neither one of us is as young as we once were, but we're lucky to have the boys close to help out."

"I should—"

"No, you shouldn't. You did enough when Dad had the stroke, including putting your life on hold and giving your all to making him better." She retrieved a pair of shoes from near the back door and took a seat on the nearest chair with a look that told Hayley that arguing wouldn't be accepted. "Now, let me get my shoes changed—" She looked at Hayley's bare feet. "You, too, and then we'll be on our way. Dad will probably be back from town before we get back from our walk, and sorry he missed it."

Within minutes, they were walking down the drive to the dirt road that ran for miles before heading into the small town where Hayley and her brothers had gone to school. "Where'd you get that?" Hayley asked her mom, eyeing the hand-carved walking stick her mother carried.

"Don't you remember me telling you about the vacation we took to Colorado?"

"Yeah, sort of."

Her mother turned to give her a look that said a lot more than words would have. "Sounds like you need to take a break."

Hayley nodded and focused on the road ahead. "You're probably right. And maybe I will after graduation, but I sure hope I can find a good clinic that will hire me as soon as possible after that."

"Are you still hoping to practice somewhere in Oklahoma City?"

Hayley nodded again but said nothing. She knew her mother's feelings on the subject, but it wasn't what she'd dreamed of when she made the decision to go into medicine.

To her relief, her mother didn't comment, much less give her a sermon on how smaller communities needed medical care more than those in the city did. And it wasn't that Hayley wasn't aware or disagreed with that, but she'd spent most of her life near a community of less than a thousand people, and she wanted more. More people, more things to do, more chances to help. There would always be people in the city who might not otherwise have access to the kind of medical treatment others normally did. If she could find a clinic in an area that catered to the less fortunate, she'd be happy to work there.

They'd walked in silence for some time, when her mother turned around to start back for the house. Hayley hadn't felt uncomfortable in the quiet. She had too many things on her mind. One of those was the way she felt about Luke and what she should do about it. She was weighing her many options, when her mother's steps slowed.

"Something is bothering you, Hayley."

Hayley pressed her lips together and tried to think of the best way to respond. "Why would you think that?"

"Maybe because I know you so well."

Telling her mom might be a way out of the mess she found herself in, but she needed to deal with these things on her own, to make her own decisions, without the input of family. She needed to be her own person. After all, she was twenty-seven years old. She hadn't been a child who needed her mother's guidance for a long time.

"There's nothing to talk about, Mom."

"Really?" A hint of sarcasm lay buried in her mother's question. "It isn't like we expected you to visit yesterday."

"It was a spur-of-the-moment decision."

"Why is that?"

At least the answer was easy. "Luke had some business to take care of in this direction, and I thought it would be nice if you met Brayden." She thought about the little boy and his fascination with the toys she'd brought him that first day. "It's a treat for him to see the cows, too. You should see him, Mom. He's always putting the cow in the back of the toy pickup I gave him that had belonged to the boys."

"He's adorable," Sharon agreed. "But why are you thinking of spending another night, after Luke and

Brayden have gone home? Why have your brother drive you back tomorrow? What good will staying here do?"

Hayley hadn't expected her change of plans to stir up so much attention, especially from her mother. She wasn't quite sure how to answer, but she had to try. "I just— I have a lot on my mind. You know, with school and the future."

"And Luke Walker and his son."

Sliding a quick look at her mother, Hayley saw that she was being closely watched. "I don't know what you mean."

"I mean, there's something going on between you and your employer."

"There's not!" Hayley immediately cried, then wished she hadn't. Her mother knew her too well, and Hayley was sure she'd now left no doubt in her mother's mind.

"Does he know?"

"I don't have a clue. Sometimes I think—"

"That he must sense something?"

"Yes, that's it! But other times…"

"What about him? Has he said anything? Done anything to let you know that he's feeling something, too?"

Hayley really didn't want tell her mother about the kiss that had nearly gotten out of control during the storm. It might have just been the letdown from the stress they'd been under or the storm that drove them together and eventually into each other's arms.

"I can't tell," she finally answered. They walked a few steps before she added, "I'm so confused. It was so easy in the beginning, but now…" She shook her head.

She didn't even know how to describe all that had happened in such a short time.

"So you haven't told him."

"No."

"Then maybe it's time you did."

Hayley stopped and turned to her mother, her heart pounding with apprehension at the very idea. "I wouldn't know what to say. And sometimes I think…"

"What?"

She met her mother's gaze. "That some morning, soon, I'll wake up and realize that we never wanted the same things."

Her mother's smile was soft and understanding. A little sad, too, in a strange way. "You can't keep doing that, Hayley. It isn't fair to him or to you. And it certainly isn't fair to that little boy."

"But—"

"Are you running away because of something that happened in the past?"

More confused than ever, Hayley tried to answer. "I don't know. Maybe knowing how he feels would make a difference." But would it? "Or maybe not."

"Then find out."

Hayley stared ahead, where she could see the farm in the distance. "All right. I'll try."

"Soon. Very soon, Hayley."

Knowing exactly what her mother meant, she nodded. "I'll let him know that I'm not staying here tonight, after all."

Her mother put an arm around her. "You'll be glad you talked to him, no matter what the outcome. Nothing is worse than not knowing. Keeping your feelings to yourself isn't fair to either of them."

Hayley knew her mother was right. Sharon Walker had always been wise, and except for the time with Nathan, Hayley had always listened. This time was no exception. "All right."

By the time they finished their walk and had returned to the farm, Luke and Brayden were waiting for them. "We probably should get going," Luke told them. "I don't want to get home too late. With Dylan gone—Well, we need to be up early tomorrow."

Hayley understood that Luke was now in charge of everything and would be doing the chores on his own. She'd been selfish not to think of that.

"Then I'll tell you both goodbye," Sharon said, bending down to give Brayden a hug and kiss. "You come back and see us again real soon, Brayden."

"See cows!"

"Yes! To see the cows." She straightened and glanced at Hayley before facing Luke. "Thanks for bringing them. We don't get to see Hayley as much as we'd like to, and it was pure pleasure to meet your son."

"The feeling is mutual," Luke replied, and put his arm around Brayden. "Are you ready?" he asked his son.

Before Brayden could answer, Hayley spoke. "I've changed my mind," she announced. "I'm going back with you."

By the look of his elevated eyebrows, it was clear Luke was surprised. "Okay," he said, slowly. "Whatever you want to do."

"Good." At least that much was settled.

But an hour later as they drove back to Desperation and Luke asked if there was some special reason she'd changed her mind, she wasn't quite ready to follow her mother's suggestion. "You're going to need to be up early in the morning, so I need to be there."

"But Chris planned to leave very early in the morning, or at least that's what he told me."

"Well, yes," she hedged, "but this way there isn't any chance I'd be late."

He was quiet for a moment. "That does make sense. Good thinking."

With no answer, she simply smiled. Maybe tomorrow she'd feel more like bringing up the subject of… What? That she'd fallen in love with him and didn't know what to do about it?

Leaning back against the headrest, she closed her eyes and prayed that somehow she'd find a way to say what needed said.

BY LATE MORNING ON FRIDAY, Luke had to admit that he would have to give in and hire some extra help. Another storm earlier in the week had meant even more work than usual—more than he could handle on his own. At least there hadn't been a loss of power, he thought, as he climbed on the utility tractor to distribute another large bale of hay to the small herd of cattle.

And then there was Hayley. She'd been acting strangely and avoiding him like the plague. He knew it was his fault, but other than apologizing, there wasn't much he could do. And who would be crazy enough to apologize for kissing someone they cared about? He finally decided to stay out of her way as much as possible, hoping her mood would pass. That didn't prove so difficult to do, thanks to the weather and the need for more help. He'd spent more time at his brother's place than he had at home.

Could that be Hayley's problem? He didn't think it was, but they'd seen so little of each other all week. When he made it home each evening, he spent as much time with Brayden as he could. Suppertime was a battle to stay awake, so once his son was in bed, Luke turned in, too. Then he was up at the crack of dawn the next day. Not exactly the best of situations.

He'd finished feeding the cattle and had started for the barn when he heard the sound of a vehicle turning into the drive.

"Well, I'll be damned."

Watching as the dark green pickup pulled in and parked close to the house, he wasn't sure if it was a good sign or a bad one. If the latter, he wasn't sure how much more he could take. For the past two months, his life had been turned upside down. Some of that was good, but this stuff with Dylan was getting to be more than he could take. Even so, he was happy to see his brother step out of the pickup, wave and head his way.

"Back already?" he asked, as Dylan drew closer.

Dylan almost smiled. "Yeah."

Luke wasn't sure what to think. "Is this a visit? Or what?"

"I'm here to stay."

Relief spread through Luke. At least he wouldn't be interviewing high school kids, who, if hired, would probably last a few days and then quit, because the work cut into their social lives. On the other hand, he worried that Dylan still hadn't dealt with his problems, and they'd be repeating this crazy cycle forever.

"I mean it, Luke," Dylan said, as if he knew what Luke was thinking. "I'm here to stay and ready to get back to work. Where do you want me to start?"

For once, Luke decided he needed to be honest, instead of simply going along with whatever Dylan said or did. "Why don't you start by telling me what's been going on with you."

Dylan stared at him, long and hard, and then finally nodded. "You're right. I owe you an explanation. Big-time."

Nodding, Luke waited. He didn't expect much. For years, Dylan hadn't been able to talk about a lot of things, yet Luke still held on to the hope that someday the devils that were chasing his brother would turn tail and run.

Dylan grabbed a nearby empty feed bucket, turned it upside down and settled on it. "It's been fifteen years since the accident," he said, without looking at Luke.

"I know."

With a shrug, Dylan continued. "I guess it's been weighing on me more, and lately it's gotten hard for me to handle."

Luke wished with all his heart that Dylan would stop blaming himself for something that had never been his fault. But he also knew that telling his brother that again would be useless.

"I saw Erin and talked to her," Dylan said.

Luke tried to hide his surprise. "What did she say?"

"She said she'd have my hide if I didn't get back here

and carry my part of the responsibilities of the ranch the way I should."

Luke wished she hadn't done that. He'd always felt that Dylan had to do what he needed to do. Keeping him on the ranch wasn't going to help. Not if it was painful for him. "Sounds just like her."

"Yeah, it did. I should've expected it." Dylan's head was lowered and he was silent for a moment. "But that wasn't all."

"Something tells me you don't like what she said."

"Nope, I sure didn't. And I still don't."

There was nothing else Luke could say except, "So what is it?"

Dylan raised his head and looked directly at him. "She thinks I should see a shrink."

Luke shouldn't have been surprised that his sister had been so honest. After all, she'd never been one to hold back or keep her opinions to herself. He wasn't exactly sure what he could say to his brother, especially since he agreed with his sister's suggestion, but maybe it was time for him to be honest, too. "So what's wrong with that?"

"I don't want someone telling me what to do."

"Erin's always been bossy," Luke pointed out.

Dylan stared at him for a moment, then shook his head. "I didn't mean her. I mean a shrink."

Now that it was out in the open, Luke didn't intend to skirt around the subject. "Might not be a bad idea."

"A shrink? Come on…"

"They don't tell you what to do," Luke hurried to say. "At least I don't think they do. Erin and I have worried about you for a long time."

Dylan was quiet. "So you think it's a good idea, too?"

"I don't see why not," Luke answered with a shrug. "You could ask Jules O'Brien. She's a psychologist. Or Paige. You trust her."

"I'll think about it."

Luke's hopes began to grow, but one look at his brother and he knew it was all for nothing. There had to be a way to help him, but if he wouldn't get help from a professional, Luke didn't know what else to tell him. "You have to do *something.*"

"I know. I just..." He pushed himself to his feet.

Luke moved away, knowing that once again, he'd failed his brother. But he had to remember that it was Dylan's problem, not his, and Dylan had to either work it out or not.

"Oh, and one other thing Erin said."

Luke stopped and turned back. "What's that?"

"She said that if I don't do something with the house, she's going to come up here and give me what for."

Luke laughed. That was Erin. She'd made a life for herself away from the ranch and the memories, but she still insisted on speaking her mind about what went on with the ranch and the family. "Did she give you any idea how to go about that?"

"Not a one. But I'm sure she'll be calling to give me some instructions." Dylan stubbed his toe in the dirt and kicked up a cloud of dust. "She had a few things to say about you, too, and I can't say I disagree."

Frowning, Luke wasn't sure if he wanted to know. He didn't particularly like the idea of his brother and sister talking about him when he wasn't there to defend himself, but he couldn't say too much. He and Erin had talked about Dylan plenty of times. Still, he was curious. "About what?"

Dylan looked up. "Hayley."

Luke didn't like his brother's smile. Instead of commenting, he shrugged and looked toward the road, wishing someone would come along and deliver something. Hayley wasn't a subject he wanted to discuss. Not with his brother. Not with anybody.

"You know," Dylan began, in a tone that Luke knew didn't bode well, "I witnessed that kiss. I just didn't say anything about it."

It was all Luke could do not to tell his brother to mind his own business. "So why bring it up now?"

"Maybe because I don't think you've done anything about it, and I think you should."

"Oh, yeah?" Luke was used to Dylan being bossy about the ranch work, but he'd never butted in about his personal life. Not even when things were bad with Kendra. "And just what do you think I should do?"

"I think you should give some serious thought to having a real relationship with her."

Luke shook his head. "Not a good idea. I'm her employer."

"Right, and nothing like that has ever happened."

"I have better things to do," Luke shot off. "Do you think this past week has been a holiday?"

"And I take the blame for that. But that doesn't mean you shouldn't do something about this thing with Hayley."

"There isn't any *thing* with Hayley!"

The corner of Dylan's mouth turned up in what appeared to be a smirk. "Sure. And now I suppose you'll say that you aren't any more attracted to her than you are to that fence post over there. Because I'm not blind. She's hot!"

Luke had had enough and took a step toward his brother, his hands fisted.

"Thanks for proving my point," Dylan said, crossing his arms on his chest.

Luke gritted his teeth. He'd fallen right into Dylan's trap. "Okay, you win," he admitted with reluctance, and hoped his brother didn't gloat. "I am attracted to her. I just don't know what it means or what to do."

"Then my advice is that you better figure it out, and fast," Dylan said, giving him a hard, brotherly pat on the back, "before somebody else beats you to her."

Luke watched Dylan walk to his pickup and pull out his duffel bag before heading for the house. As he stepped up onto the porch, he stopped and turned back. "Don't let any grass grow under your feet, bro. More'n likely it'll be crabgrass."

Luke didn't answer. As he watched Dylan walk into the house, he had a feeling his brother was right. But just what could he do? He didn't have any idea how Hayley felt about him. She'd steered clear of him after that latest kiss. But she hadn't quit. Maybe that was a good sign. And maybe he needed to find out for sure.

HAYLEY PULLED THE CAR into one of the empty spaces in the parking lot of the city park. Kate had called her the day after she'd returned from visiting her parents and invited her to join them in a weekly play day for the kids. Hayley was excited. Brayden needed more interaction with other children. He'd spent far too much time on the ranch without playmates.

After helping Brayden from his car seat, the two of them walked hand in hand to the playground where the other three children were playing. "Look, Brayden," she told him when they were closer, "there's your new friends. Do you want to go play with Tyler and Travis and Krista?"

Brayden tipped his head up to see her, his expression announcing his uncertainty. But when Travis called to him, a slow smile began transforming his face, and he soon was running toward them.

"Glad you two could make it," Trish said, when Hayley joined them on the park bench. "These kids need new blood. Being cousins and the same age, they see way too much of each other."

"No kidding," Kate immediately agreed. "Sometimes I wonder if one of us should move away."

Trish's mouth dropped open. "Then that will have to be you, because Morgan and I have no intention of leaving Desperation."

"Well, if you think Dusty and I are going to move, you have another think coming."

The twinkle in the eyes of both women contradicted their tone and their words. "Now, ladies," Hayley said, laughing. "I think Desperation is big enough for both of you. And I want to thank you for inviting us today. The last time we were here with you, Brayden couldn't stop talking about the two boys and the girl he'd played with. I lost count of how many times he told Luke, who did a great job of pretending each time that he hadn't heard the story a dozen times before."

"The sign of an excellent father," Trish announced. "Grab him up before some other woman does, Hayley."

Although Hayley knew Trish was joking and she laughed with the two women, it was one more reminder of what a great guy Luke was. From the very first day, he'd proven over and over again that he was a super dad, something she hadn't noticed an abundance of. Her dad was unequaled when it came to caring for his kids, but she'd seen too many men who were too busy or didn't know what to do with their children.

Even with the knowledge that it would be hard to find another man who cared so much for his son and had many of the qualities women look for in a husband, as Luke did, she hadn't come to the point where she could tell him how she felt. After she'd learned her lesson with Nathan, she'd given up and focused on her career. She'd become known for telling-it-like-it-is. But for some reason, she couldn't even begin to do the telling, when it came to Luke.

Hayley turned at the sound of a car approaching.

"Hey, Paige," Kate called to the doctor, who had parked her car and was headed toward them. "What brings you to the park?"

Dr. O'Brien joined them at the edge of the playground. "I was headed home for a quick lunch, saw your cars and decided to stop. Are we still on for Saturday?"

"Definitely," Trish answered and glanced at her sister. "But it's a week from this Saturday, right? I mean we talked about it the other day."

Kate nodded. "We'll be there. What about you?"

The doctor's smile widened. "I wouldn't miss it."

Feeling as if she was eavesdropping on something private, Hayley started to walk toward the small slide where the four children were playing.

"Hayley?" Kate called to her.

She stopped and looked back over her shoulder. "Just checking on Brayden."

"Well, come on back. The kids are doing fine."

Hayley made a quick cursory check on Brayden, and then returned to the park bench. "He gets braver by the day, but he's having so much fun, I hate to caution him too much."

"They do enjoy coming to the park," Trish agreed. "Besides, now that Paige is here, we have a doctor, in case something should happen. Although I really doubt she'll be needed," she added quickly.

"Two doctors," Dr. O'Brien said.

"Two?"

"Hayley is an RN *and* studying to be a physician's assistant," the doctor explained, "so she's almost as good as a doctor."

Embarrassed, Hayley quickly amended the statement. "Not even close, Dr. O'Brien."

"It's Paige, please. And I'm glad you're here. I was thinking of giving you a call. Our head nurse is retiring."

"Oh, no!" Trish cried. "Not Susan."

"I'm afraid so. She and Don have been hoping to do some traveling before, as she puts it, they're too old to enjoy it." She turned to place a hand on Hayley's arm. "I could really use another nurse. I do wish you'd consider taking the position."

Hayley had liked Desperation's doctor as soon as

she'd met her, and she also understood the difficulties of being understaffed. But making a decision like that was more than she was ready to do. "I really can't give you an answer, Dr.— I mean Paige," she corrected with a smile. "Not right now."

"I understand," Paige said, with an obviously staged sigh, and then added a smile. "But think about it. We're still hoping to enlarge the clinic in the near future, so there could very well be a position open for you as a PA, later on."

Smiling, Hayley nodded. "Right now I'm focusing on graduating. And, too, I haven't really made plans to stay on in Desperation after that."

"Really?" Trish asked.

Now Hayley wished she hadn't said anything. Not knowing what might happen, when and if she could work up the nerve to talk to Luke, making decisions about anything wasn't just difficult, it was foolish. "I don't have any plans yet," she explained. "But for now, I have to say it would be better not to count on me for the job. I'm sorry. I'm sure the clinic is a great place to work."

There was no denying that Paige was disappointed, by the look on her face, but she smiled. "I understand, Hayley. I really do. I didn't start out in a small town, either. But if you should change your mind, you know where to find me."

"I do," Hayley answered, feeling bad that she couldn't be more certain.

Kate placed a hand on her arm. "No matter what you decide, maybe you'd like to join us for our Girls Night Out a week from Saturday. Actually, it's in the afternoon, but it's our time to get together and have some fun."

"Oh, I don't know," Hayley hedged. "Saturdays are busy on the ranch, so I usually spend the day with Brayden."

"We'd love to have you," Trish added.

Hayley smiled. "Thank you. All of you. Maybe another time?"

"We'll make sure of it," Kate assured her.

By the time she and Brayden were on their way home again, Hayley was even more confused than she had been. She'd found Desperation to be a charming town, and the people in it friendly and helpful. It would be an ideal spot to work and maybe settle down. Once again, she was reminded that there were things she needed to say to Luke. If only she knew what and how to say them.

When her phone rang, she pulled it from her purse and noticed her mother's number. "Hi, Mom," she said, after punching the connect button and hoping she sounded normal, if not cheerful.

"I just thought I'd check to see how you're doing. Have you talked to him yet?"

Hayley had known it was coming, and she knew what her mother was going to say. "Not exactly," she hedged, wishing she'd never told her mother what was going on in her life.

The sound her mother made told her she was in for a lecture, something she hadn't endured for a long, long time. And she wasn't looking forward to it.

Chapter Eleven

Luke took his attention off the highway ahead long enough to look at Hayley in the passenger seat beside him. “This is a lot better than the last time we drove into the city.”

“Definitely,” she answered, leaning her head back and smiling. “That wasn’t something a parent ever wants to experience.”

“But we made it through okay.”

“We did.”

“Thanks to you.”

“I didn’t do anything, Luke,” she replied, turning her head to look at him. “You were the one who was there in the hospital with Brayden.”

“And you were the one who stayed calm.” The Friday-evening traffic was heavy on the way into Oklahoma City, but he managed another glance at her when she didn’t answer.

She shrugged and looked straight ahead. “Anybody would have done the same.”

He didn’t agree, but he was determined not to argue with her. She’d been in a strange mood for the past two weeks, and he’d made sure to give her a wide berth. That hadn’t been easy.

"So where are we going?" she asked.

"I was thinking dinner and a movie. Or a movie and dinner."

"Or just dinner?"

"Sure. Whatever you want." He knew what he wanted, but he also knew it wasn't his for the taking. Not even if he asked. But tonight could be a start. At least that was the way he was looking at it.

"I heard there was a new restaurant," she said. "Nothing fancy, great food and some of the best beer around."

"Yeah?"

Her laughter filled the interior of the truck. "Yeah."

Twenty minutes later they were waiting in line to get a table. The place was packed, and Luke guessed it would be at least another thirty minutes before they'd have the chance to check out the food everyone around them kept talking about.

"I'm so sorry," Hayley said, stepping out of the way as a new group of people came in the door.

He was forced to move even closer to her and didn't really mind. "Nothing to be sorry about," he assured her. "Besides, we're not in a hurry, are we?"

She squeezed farther into the corner, when the door opened again. "Only if you think there might be a problem for Dylan."

Luke shook his head, trying to make a little extra room for her. "He's the one who offered to take Brayden for the night." He wasn't going to tell her that the whole evening had been his brother's idea. And Dylan wouldn't take no for an answer, although Luke hadn't been real keen on the idea at first. Now he was glad his brother had insisted.

"I'll have to remember to thank—"

He not only noticed that she didn't finish her sentence, but that she was staring at the latest group of people to enter. "Hayley?"

When she didn't answer, he tried to see what had caught her attention. Or who. He wasn't sure. And then he heard a female voice call her name.

"Is that really you?" The woman—young, tall and blond—was only a few feet away, but the small waiting area was so crowded, moving in any direction promised to be almost life-threatening.

"Yes, it's me," Hayley replied. "What a crush, huh?"

"Oh, it always is."

"Who are you talking to, Marianne?" a male voice asked.

Luke felt Hayley's body stiffen next to him. One quick look at her face, suddenly pale, told him there was something about the man who'd spoken that bothered her. And Luke was curious. Real curious.

"Table for Walker."

Before he had a chance to move, Hayley waved at the blonde. "Great to see you again, Marianne!" Then she turned to him and slipped her hand into the crook of his arm. "I thought they'd never have a table for us."

He chanced a look at her, and didn't fail to catch the hard glitter in her eyes as she smiled up at him. Something was definitely up.

They made their way to their table and were immediately joined by a waiter, who left them with menus, and soon after was followed by a waitress who took their orders.

"That was fast," Luke said, when he and Hayley were alone.

"Amazing, considering the crowd here tonight." She went on to tell him that the blonde she'd spoken to had been a classmate in college, but she didn't mention the man, and Luke didn't ask.

When the waitress arrived with their drinks, he had a feeling they were in trouble. "Uh-oh, that's one gigantic margarita," he said, indicating Hayley's huge glass with a nod.

She looked up as the waitress placed it in front of her. "You're kidding, right?"

The waitress laughed and shook her head. "The menu *does* say very large." She grinned at Luke, adding a conspiratorial wink. "But don't worry if you can't finish it. Lots of people don't."

"I'm not surprised," Hayley replied.

When the waitress disappeared, Luke stared at the size of the drink. "Maybe they give a prize or something to those who can finish."

Chuckling, Hayley took a sip. "If that's the case, I'll be going home empty-handed."

They changed the subject and talked about Brayden and Dylan's return. When their order arrived, their talk turned to favorite food. Luke was surprised that she, like he, enjoyed the simpler things more than the exotic. "Maybe because we were both country kids," he suggested.

Just as she started to answer, the man who'd caused what he could only call her earlier discomfort approached their table with a very young woman. "You're looking good, Hayley, but I hadn't heard you'd taken up drinking," the man said, stopping next to her chair.

Luke watched as her eyes narrowed and she looked up. The smile on her face didn't match her eyes, and he hoped he never had the bad luck to have her look at him that way.

"They get a bit carried away," she said, her gaze moving toward the woman, her smile more congenial. "Great for a little celebrating, though."

"Celebrating?" the man asked, glancing at Luke as if he was an uninvited guest. Then a practiced smile appeared and he held out his hand. "Nathan Hardy."

Luke took the offered hand. "Luke Walker."

The young woman giggled. "Is your middle name Sky?"

Luke got the joke immediately. He'd heard the same question since he was old enough to remember, though he hadn't been born when the first movie premiered. Even so, both he and Dylan had become fans at a young age. "No, ma'am," he answered, and her cheeks reddened. "But you're not the first to ask," he added to soften the blow.

She ducked her head, and then looped her arm through her date's. "Maybe we should be getting back to our table," she said, looking up with wide eyes and a childish pout at the man.

Across the table, Luke noticed Hayley's quick grimace, and he nearly laughed. It didn't take a whole lot to guess what was going on, but he wasn't going to let on that he'd figured it out, unless Hayley brought it up.

"Yes, you're probably right." Nathan Hardy's arm

snaked around her as he smiled, first at Luke and then at Hayley. "Enjoy your drink," he told her. "Just don't get into any trouble."

Luke watched them walk away, before asking, "He a friend of yours?"

She sniffed. "Not at all," she announced, and then took a long drink.

As far as Luke was concerned, if she wanted to drink herself silly, he wasn't going to stop her. She obviously felt she had reason, and it was probably none of his business what that reason was. But that didn't stop him from being curious, even though he reminded himself that asking would be rude.

"She was kind of young," he commented, instead, to see her reaction.

Across the table, a very tipsy Hayley snorted. "The younger they are, the easier to control, my dear."

Surprised, Luke didn't answer as she took another long drink. Reaching across the table, he wrapped his fingers around the fat stem of the big margarita glass and pulled it away from her. "Why don't we head home?"

Hayley closed her eyes and nodded. "You're right. I've had more than enough tonight."

He hoped to avoid the table where her friends were sitting, but it wasn't possible. As they passed by, Hayley raised her hand to wiggle her fingers in a wave and tell them, "Bye-bye."

She seemed okay from all the drinking, as they walked to his pickup, although she was very quiet. She remained quiet for some time, as he drove through the traffic that thinned as they left the city behind. When he'd had enough quiet, he finally decided to say something, even though he didn't expect her to answer.

"Is something bothering you, Hayley?"

She turned in the seat to look at him. "You're going to regret asking me that, you know."

Normally, he would have laughed, but because of the look on her face, he wondered if she might be right.

A LITTLE VOICE IN Hayley's head told her she'd be better off if she kept quiet. She knew she'd had too much to drink. The last time she'd come within a foot of an alcoholic beverage, she'd made a fool of herself at the wedding of her oldest brother. Would she ever learn?

"I don't drink very often," she began, thankful for the cover of darkness. "In fact, after the last time I embarrassed myself and my family, I swore I wouldn't do it again."

"How long ago was that?"

She closed her eyes as the memory shot through her. "Three years ago, at Chris's wedding."

"Your oldest brother."

She nodded, then realized he couldn't see her. "Yes."

"Okay. So what about tonight?"

"It was silly, really."

"It usually is."

She obviously wasn't going to get out of explaining herself. The more she thought about it, the more she wondered if telling wouldn't be such a bad thing. It was all in the past and couldn't hurt her again. Besides, he deserved to know, although she couldn't for the life of her remember why.

She took a deep breath before answering. "That man? The one who stopped by our table?"

There was a beat of silence before Luke replied. "With the young woman—the very young woman."

"Yes, that man." She wished with all her heart that they'd gone somewhere else. If they had, she'd probably be thinking clearly, instead of trying to figure out which words were the right ones to say. She was definitely having a problem with that.

"An old boyfriend?" Luke asked.

"Sort of," she hedged. The sound of the tires on the pavement beneath them seemed to grow louder as she waited for him to say something. When he didn't, she knew she'd begun this crazy idea to tell him what happened, and she couldn't just stop now. "We were once engaged."

She felt more than saw him turn his head to look at her. "Engaged? To be married?"

Unsure of what to say, she simply replied with, "That would be it."

"He left you for a younger woman."

He sounded convinced that he'd guessed correctly, and her sigh filled the cab of the pickup. For a moment, she felt dizzy, as her thoughts swirled in her mind, but she managed to right them again. "If only that had been the problem."

"Do you plan to tell me what was?"

She gritted her teeth on the giggle that threatened to escape and wondered why it seemed so funny now, so many years later. Just talking about it again made her feel vulnerable. Or maybe it was the drink. Either way, she didn't really like the feeling.

"I suppose I owe you that much," she admitted. "I met Nathan during my second year of college. I guess you could say he swept me off my feet."

A quiet noise that resembled a grunt came from the other side of the truck. "And then?"

"We became engaged, and after I finished classes that spring, he suggested that I might want to postpone my education for a semester or two so I could focus on planning our wedding. At the time, it sounded reasonable."

"And now?"

She shrugged her shoulders, wishing she could just close her eyes and go to sleep. She didn't care about all the things that had happened with Nathan. It had been a long time ago, and seeing him again didn't arouse any of those old feelings she'd been afraid she might still have for him.

"Now I know it was all a lie," she answered. "It was probably a good thing I decided to take some time off, because my dad suffered a stroke, and I needed to be there to help my mom."

"I've suspected you've always been a responsible person. But your dad got better, right?"

"After a while, yes." She remembered how hard that time was for her mother and how frustrated her dad became when his progress didn't move faster. But he was fine now. Even the paralysis in his right side had pretty much gone away.

She suddenly realized that Luke was waiting for her to tell him more, so she hurried on, ready to finish the story. Maybe then she could sleep. "In the meantime," she continued, "I started seeing things in Nathan that bothered me. In the end, I realized the truth. He never wanted me to have a career. Everything would have been fine if I'd just been the happy little homemaker. That wasn't what I wanted—or want now—so I ended it."

"Better sooner than later."

Mixed with the little bit of regret in Luke's voice was the hard edge she'd heard when he spoke of his ex-wife. "So here we are," she said, as cheerfully as her muddled mind would allow.

"Yes, we are."

"What?" She focused out the windshield ahead and realized they'd left the paved road behind and were now turning onto the drive of Luke's ranch. "Oh, we're home."

"Right." He drove off to the left and parked the truck, instead of driving into the garage as he usually would have done. "I left some papers in the barn. Sit tight, and I'll be right back."

She wasn't sure how long she sat there, her head leaned back against the seat, as a mixed bag of memories did somersaults in her mind. Instead of fighting them, she hoped they'd slow down so she wouldn't feel quite so dizzy.

"Hayley?"

She heard her name and felt a breeze on her face, but she thought they were just a part of the crazy acrobatics in her head. And then she felt the touch on her arm. "What?"

"Let's get you into the house."

She recognized Luke's voice and forced her eyes

open to see him standing in the open pickup door. "We're home."

He chuckled. "Yeah, we are. Here, let me help you out."

The air held a bit of a chill, and her mind cleared a little. She gave him her hand when he held out his and immediately noticed the feeling of warm honey flowing through her. Be careful, she reminded herself, and she didn't mean getting out of the truck. *Once burned, twice shy.*

After swinging her legs around, she slid down to the ground, and Luke stepped back, giving her room. A bit befuddled by what she guessed was the shortest nap in history, made worse by the alcohol she'd had earlier, she started for the house. She heard him close the pickup door, then the sound of his steps in the yard as he followed her.

"Watch out for the—"

She tripped in the dark, falling hard to her knees, and let out a cry of surprise and pain.

"Tree root," he finished.

Before she could even discover how badly she was hurt, or even if she had been, he was leaning down to help her to her feet. "I know better," she said, on a little hiccup.

He held both of her hands as she stood perfectly still in front of him. He was so close she could hear his every breath. She forgot about her knees, except that they weren't doing a very good job of holding her up, and somehow she knew it wasn't because she'd fallen on them. Oh, she'd fallen, all right, but a tree root wasn't to blame. And it wasn't her knees she was worried about.

Still holding her hands, he moved them to reach behind her back, bringing her closer to him, and she sighed, unable to fight for the sanity she desperately needed.

"Hayley..."

A shiver of heat went through her, and she arched her back, pressing closer to him as he gently held her. Before she could even consider protesting, she felt his mouth on hers. Instead of invading, as he easily could have, he kissed her gently, tentatively. In the back of her mind, she knew it was wrong, but it felt so good, as if every bone in her body was melting, that she ignored the whispered warning and went about silencing it.

The touch of his tongue dragged a moan from her. Not only was her mind weak and numbed by the earlier alcohol, but also by the tantalizing things her body was now experiencing.

At some point he released her hands from behind her back and pulled her even closer, pressing her hard against him. In response, her arms went up and around his neck. She groaned into his mouth when he delved deeper with his tongue, and all thought vanished, except for a whisper that maybe this wasn't such a good idea. It was gone in a heartbeat, lost in a fog of passion.

She wasn't sure how long they'd been locked in the embrace when her stomach gave the first indication that things weren't going well. It took every bit of strength she had to pull away from what she had guessed might be a little bit of heaven.

"What?" he whispered, when they were inches apart.

"I—" She shook her head and shoved at his chest with her hands.

"Hayley? What—"

"Sick." After that, she didn't remember much of anything, except stumbling through the yard and hoping he didn't follow, then the occasional wish that the ground would open up and swallow her. She wasn't sure it didn't.

It was much later when she opened her eyes to mere slits. She tried desperately to avoid anything that would make her head hurt much more than it already did. Without meaning to, she moved, and a low groan escaped her lips.

What had she done that made her feel so bad?

Squeezing her eyes shut against the onslaught of memories and sensations didn't make the situation any better. She was mortified that she'd participated in the lovemaking, completely aware that it had been cut short because she'd had far too much to drink. Still it had exceeded her wildest dreams. It wouldn't have taken much prompting for her to have gone to bed with her employer.

Her employer! The father of the little boy who had been entrusted to her care.

The clearer her mind became as to what had transpired, the more convinced she was that she could no longer continue her job. If she couldn't trust herself to act in a professional manner at all times, she had no choice but to issue her resignation as Brayden's nanny. And she suspected that wouldn't go over very well with Luke. While she didn't believe he'd formed any deep feelings for her, unlike the ones she had for him, finding someone to take her place might not be easy. But neither would leaving Brayden—and him—be easy for her.

If only she had talked to him as her mother had suggested. But she hadn't.

LUKE SLAMMED THE GEARSHIFT into Park, flipped off the key in the ignition then let out a stream of words he hoped his son would never hear when he rammed his shoulder into the door while trying to get out of his pickup. Gritting his teeth at the pain, he managed to open the door and was soon sprinting up the steps of his house, wondering how he'd managed to get himself in the mess he suspected he was now in.

A glance at his watch as he threw open the front door told him he was in for some real trouble. If he thought Hayley had been upset before when he'd been late on a night she had her class, he had a feeling he hadn't experienced the worst. But he probably would, as soon as he could find her.

He spied her in the kitchen and headed her way, hoping she'd let him explain. "Before you say anything, I'm—"

"It doesn't matter."

He stopped in his tracks. Of course it mattered. He was almost thirty minutes later than he should have been. Just one look at her was enough to tell him that she would probably never forgive him. He didn't blame her. He'd acted shamefully on Friday night, taking advantage of her when she was vulnerable. As her employer, he'd been so far out of line that she had every right to be upset...and more. He wished he'd been able to think of the words he'd needed to tell her that he would do whatever it took to make things right with her. Instead, he'd given her a wide berth over the weekend. And now this.

When she'd asked for the day off on Sunday, he'd immediately said yes. But the entire time she was gone, he wondered where she'd been, worried that he'd caused irreparable damage to their relationship, whatever that relationship had been. He wasn't sure of anything anymore. He hadn't been since Brayden's stay in the hospital.

But it was Monday now, and he'd planned to either tackle the problem or move past it. If he told her why he was late, it might make a difference. After all, it wasn't his fault that Ned Porter had dumped half his trailer of round bales in the middle of the road. Then there was the gash on Ned's leg that had needed attention, so a call to the fire station for an ambulance was needed, and being unable to get past the trailer and home—

"It's Monday," she said, without looking his way, "so would it be possible to get my paycheck now?"

Taken by surprise at her request, instead of being read the riot act for being late, he hurried to answer. "Sure. I made it out yesterday. Be right back."

It wasn't until he had the check in hand and had started back to the kitchen that he noticed the boxes and suitcases near the door that led to the garage.

"What are these?" he asked, stopping and pointing at them.

"My things," she answered, without looking up at him.

His blood suddenly ran cold through his veins,

and he had to force himself to speak. "What kind of things?"

She opened the refrigerator and took out a bottle of water. Without looking in his direction and focusing instead on opening the bottle, she said, "My things. My clothes and my belongings."

Determined not to think the worst, he returned to the kitchen and took a seat, but couldn't bring himself to look at her. "Maybe you should tell me what's going on."

"Yes, maybe I should."

Something in her voice made him look up. For a brief moment, he realized how vulnerable she was, but she quickly drew herself up and squared her shoulders, as if getting ready to do battle or something.

"I've decided it would be best if I don't stay at the ranch any longer."

He knew he shouldn't be surprised, but the sudden dread he felt put him on guard. "You have, huh?"

She looked him squarely in the eye. "Yes, I have."

Something about her—her voice or the way she stood straight and tall—poked at him like a stick. "Should I ask what brought you to this decision?"

Her throat worked as she swallowed. "I think we both have a pretty good idea."

"You mean Friday night?"

"That's part of it."

Convinced this was nothing but her emotional reaction to what had happened, he chose to use logic. "There's no reason to let the other night change anything. We can talk about it later, if you think we need to. As for tonight, I have a valid reason for being late."

She opened her mouth, as if to argue, but quickly closed it and shook her head. When she did finally speak, her gaze went right past him. "I'm sure that's the way you see it."

He immediately took exception to her tone of voice and suddenly found himself on the defensive. "There were two of us there, as I remember it."

Now she did look at him. "I'm perfectly aware of that."

"Good," he said, relieved that they agreed. Now they could put the whole incident in the past and get back to life as it should be. "I'll take your things back upstairs for you."

"No."

He felt the tic in the corner of his mouth, a sure sign that his temper might soon get the better of him. He took a deep breath, ready to say whatever was needed to make her see reason.

But Hayley obviously didn't intend to be reasonable, as she moved around the counter and stood in front of him. "I take the blame for my part in what happened Friday night and that I insisted on living here from the beginning, in spite of the fact that you had doubts about it. Because of that and the fact that you're home too late for me to bother going to class, I feel it's my responsibility to make the necessary changes."

The cold dread he'd felt became icy anger. "And I suppose you've made some kind of a decision that involves moving out."

She nodded. "I'll be living elsewhere, but I'll continue to care for Brayden, until you can make other arrangements."

Anger wasn't something he experienced very often, but at that moment, he was filled with it. "And if I ask you not to do this?"

Shrugging, she turned away. "I don't intend to change my mind or the plans I've had to make."

He shot to his feet, bumping the counter hard enough to make the glasses on it rattle. "No one made you change anything. No one except you. You didn't *have* to change anything. A little thought, a little discussion with me about this, and maybe we could work this out. Instead, you made a decision that not only affects me, but my son." In that moment, he knew that this came down to Brayden, not him, and he couldn't let her walk away. "Did you even think about him?"

He heard a sigh, then noticed that all the fight seemed to have gone out of her. "Of course I thought of Brayden," she replied. "But I also have to think of myself."

"Seems to me that's all you've been doing."

She spun around, her eyes flashing with anger. "Do you think I'm so coldhearted that I haven't agonized over leaving him?"

He knew she'd formed a strong bond with Brayden, but he couldn't admit it, couldn't show weakness, so he shrugged and said nothing.

Her expression hardened, as her mouth turned down in a firm line. "You've never understood that I never planned to stay here permanently. Even as hard as it will be for me to leave Brayden, once I have my degree and have obtained a position with a doctor, I won't be here, anyway. I told you that. But like Nathan, you think women don't deserve a career."

"That's not true!"

She gave a halfhearted lift of one shoulder. "Maybe not, but it changes nothing."

She walked past him without even a glance, headed for the door at the other end of the large room. He followed her, determined to put a stop to this craziness.

"I'll be back in a couple of hours," she announced when she stopped to pick up a folded paper on top of one of the boxes. Without a word, she handed it to him.

"What's this?" he asked, taking it from her and unfolding it.

"My written resignation. As you can see, I'll continue as Brayden's nanny until you find someone else, but I won't be living here. I also included a list of possible day care options that I've checked on."

Her voice was so matter-of-fact that he might have been surprised if he hadn't been so angry that she hadn't bothered to even discuss this with him in advance. Just like Kendra, she was walking out on Brayden.

"You're free to leave, anytime," he said, barely able to form words. "And there's no time like the present. Just don't come back. Brayden and I will be fine." He tossed the paper she'd given him to the top of the boxes.

She stared at him, her eyes wide and her face pale. "All right, then."

He heard the wobble in her voice, and when she moved to pick up the paper, her hand trembled. At that moment, he didn't care. All he knew was that he hurt. Brayden would hurt even more.

Turning, he left her at the door and vowed to never let another woman hurt him or his son again.

Chapter Twelve

"I don't know how to thank you and Kate for helping me find an apartment," Hayley told the older woman with the short, white hair.

Her gray eyes sparkling, Hettie Lambert dismissed the thanks with a wave of her hand, her thin bangle bracelets giving a soft jingle. "When Aggie Clayborne told me her niece had a friend looking for a place to live, I was happy the Commune had a vacancy."

"It's only temporary."

Hettie patted her arm. "Temporary or permanent, we're glad you're here. And Ernie brought in some furniture for you, right?"

Hayley nodded, wishing circumstances were different, but knowing she hadn't had a choice except to leave Luke's home. "I really appreciate everything everyone is doing. I can't begin to repay you all."

"There's no reason to. Now, what else can we help you with?"

"I can't think of anything," Hayley answered. It was as truthful as she could be. She still felt the sting of Luke's parting words, and she missed Brayden so much that she physically ached, but she knew from experience that time would take care of both.

"Good. But if there's anything you need—anything at all—let me know. I do have a little pull in this town," Hettie added with a wink.

Hayley assured her she would remember, thanked her again and headed to the apartment she'd rented from Ernie Dolan. Located in what had formerly been the Shadybrook Retirement Home, it had recently expanded with apartments for singles. She'd learned from Kate that the tenants and then the townspeople had long ago affectionately nicknamed it the Commune, and Hayley hadn't needed to ask why. She couldn't ever remember meeting so many people in one place who were eager to welcome her and offer help with anything.

But she shouldn't have been surprised. That was the way it was in Desperation. Sure, there were the same drawbacks of small-town living, but in Desperation, there were more positives. With a little encouragement from her new friends, she'd even started to give some thought to staying there and rethinking her plan to find a position in the city.

When a knock on her door interrupted her thoughts and her pitiful attempt at decorating on less than a shoestring budget, she opened it to find Kate. "Time for lunch! Let's go down to the Chick-a-Lick and grab a bite."

Hayley laughed. "You sound like your husband."

"Proof that he's grown on me, I guess," Kate replied with an unladylike snort. "Come on, put on your shoes and let's go."

Taking a step back, Hayley shook her head. "I don't want to risk running into Luke."

Kate planted her hands on her hips and frowned.

"Are you going to let him dictate where you go and what you do?"

"Well, he isn't really dictating, exactly."

Throwing her hands in the air, Kate let out an exaggerated breath. "You can't spend every minute in this apartment. Besides, what better way is there to show him that you've moved on than to be seen out and about?"

Hayley considered it. In a short time, she'd come to like and admire Kate Clayborne McPherson. From things she'd heard, she suspected Kate didn't let anyone dictate anything to her. Not even her husband, Dusty, who everyone knew worshipped her.

"All right," Hayley said, giving in with a laugh. "Let's do lunch at the Chick-a-Lick, and to blazes with anyone who tries to stop us."

"Now you're talking!"

Forty-five minutes later, as they finished their lunch, Kate moved her plate out of the way, folded her arms on the table and leaned forward. "Paige is really shorthanded at the doctor's office. Have you given any more thought to taking her up on her offer of a job there?"

Hayley avoided her intense gaze. "A little."

"And?"

Shaking her head, Hayley sighed. "I don't know."

Kate leaned back in the booth, clearly exasperated. "Because you might run into Luke?"

Fearing someone might have heard, Hayley glanced around the café. But those who were left from the earlier crowd weren't paying a bit of attention to the two women in the back booth. "Not so much."

"You know, working there now, before you have

your degree, doesn't mean you have to stay there forever," Kate said. "You can always take a PA position in the city. You wouldn't be locked in here in Desperation."

Hayley nodded. "You're right, but I'm just not sure what I want to do."

"Working with Paige as one of her nurses might be the best way to help you decide. You'll either discover that you can't stand small-town clinics or that it's exactly what you've always wanted but didn't realize it."

Hayley smiled. Kate made a good point. "You have something there. And with having to pay rent now, I could sure use the money."

"Then you'll at least give it more thought?"

Hayley's smile widened. "Yes, I definitely will."

They finished their lunch, stopped at the cash register near the counter to pay their tab and chatted for a few minutes with the café's manager.

"We haven't seen much of you," Darla told Hayley.

Hayley glanced at Kate before answering. "Maybe I'll make it a habit to stop in, now that I'm living at the Commune."

Darla's smile didn't reveal if she knew anything about what had happened with Luke, nor did she ask. "That's great! We not only welcome your patronage, but it's even nicer to have a new friend."

Hayley thanked Darla for making her feel like a part of the community. As she and Kate stepped out the door and onto the sidewalk, Hayley spied a small boy down the street and immediately thought it was Brayden. When she realized it wasn't him, disappointment filled her and she began to wonder how things were going.

Had Luke found someone to watch over Brayden or was he keeping the little boy with him all the time?

She turned to Kate and kept her voice low. "Have you heard how things are going with Brayden?"

Kate nodded as they approached her car. "He's in day care."

Hayley was surprised. It hadn't been that long since Luke had mentioned there were no openings. "Oh! Something opened up then?"

Reaching the car, Kate glanced up as she opened the door. "Yeah. You could say that."

Hayley had opened her door, but didn't get in. "What does that mean?"

Shrugging, Kate looked at her over the top of the car. "Before you were even moved into your apartment, Luke called to ask if I'd heard about any openings or anyone who might be willing to do some babysitting, even part-time. I didn't, but I told him I'd ask around."

When Kate climbed into the car, Hayley did, too. On one hand, she knew that taking Brayden along to do the ranching wasn't the best way to raise a child. On the other hand, she was surprised and a bit disappointed that Luke had found her replacement so quickly.

"So you found something," she said, as Kate started the car.

"Well..."

"Well?"

Kate slowly turned her head to look at Hayley. "I called Libby and asked for a favor."

Hayley took a deep breath before asking, "Libby?"

"She runs the new day care in town. Haven't you met her?"

"Not that I remember."

"Then you need to. She's a very special woman, who came here with her son when they were on the run from her abusive ex-husband."

"How awful!" Hayley could only imagine what that might be like.

Putting the car in gear, Kate backed out of the parking spot. "It all turned out okay. Libby and Garrett Miles were married on New Year's Day. Garrett is not only the city attorney, but Paige's brother." She glanced at Hayley. "You might want to know that before you take that nursing job."

"You're awfully certain that I'm going to work there."

Kate shrugged and stepped on the gas. "I know we haven't known each other very long, but in the short time we have, you strike me as an intelligent, giving woman. And unless you have something waiting for you right now, Paige's offer is a good one. You'd be a fool to pass it up."

Hayley couldn't argue with that. Besides, if she hadn't planned on staying in Desperation, why had she rented an apartment? The truth was she liked it in Desperation. Really liked it. If it wasn't for the problem of running into Luke, Desperation would be the perfect place for her.

So why was she giving him so much power over her decision to stay?

The question was the answer, and she leaned back in the seat, smiling. "Would you mind dropping me off at the doctor's office, Kate? There's something I need to do."

"HEY! WATCH WHERE YOU'RE throwing those things."

The sound of Dylan's voice caused Luke to look up and see his brother standing on the end of the hay trailer, hands on hips and a frown on his face. Round bales of hay were stacked behind him, along with the smaller, rectangular bales Luke was tossing up with the others. As soon as all of them were loaded, the bales would be taken to a neighbor, who'd lost his supply when lightning struck his hay shed.

"Sorry," Luke replied, then turned to grab the wire that held another bale together. He knew he should have his mind on what he was doing, but he hadn't had much luck since Hayley had walked out five days before.

"Hold on, will ya?" Dylan shouted, stopping Luke from heaving another bale at him. "Maybe we need to take a break. It's getting close to lunchtime. Why don't we clean up a little and grab a bite at the Chick-a-Lick?"

Luke didn't have any desire to go into Desperation. Even though he'd always enjoyed going to the local café, he preferred having lunch with Hayley and Brayden. But his son was spending the day with Dusty's twin boys, and Hayley was— *Gone.* Hayley was gone, thanks to him.

"Nah," he answered. "Just bring me back something to eat."

Dylan jumped down from the trailer. "Nope. I'm not bringing anything back. If you want to eat, you have to come with me."

Luke started to argue, but thought better of it. He didn't have an excuse Dylan would accept, so he shrugged and pulled off his work gloves. "Okay, I'll go."

Dylan gave him a sound smack on the back, before

taking off for the house. With a grunt of resignation Luke followed.

He'd tried to keep from thinking about Hayley, but it wasn't easy. Brayden had taken to checking the upstairs bedroom and the downstairs one, too, and it nearly broke Luke's heart when he saw the sadness in his son's eyes when he found both empty. He couldn't even watch Brayden play with his toys, without thinking of how close he might have come to losing him. Hayley had stepped in and taken over, with ease and assurance.

She'd come to mean a lot to both of them, and it was hard for him to believe that he'd almost not hired her because she was too pretty. Too pretty! As if she wasn't smart and generous and everything a man with common sense could ask for in a woman. And he'd let her get away.

The café was almost at capacity when Luke and Dylan arrived, but they found a small table along the back wall. It wasn't long before they both knew what they wanted to order, but it was so busy, they had to wait for the waitress to work her way to their table. They didn't mind. Saturday at the café was their chance to catch up on the news and talk to friends.

"Busy today," Dylan commented.

Luke agreed with a nod, but said nothing.

"Hey, boys. What can I get you?" the waitress asked, when she finally reached their table.

"Looks like they're keeping you on your toes today, Wendy," Dylan said when they'd both given her their orders.

"It's been like this for the past hour." She turned

to Luke. "Where's that nice lady you've been bringing with you?"

"She, uh..." He glanced at Dylan, hoping for a little help, but his brother acted like he didn't notice. Disgusted that his own flesh and blood wouldn't come to his aid, he managed to think of an answer that would end any speculation about Hayley. "Brayden's going to Libby's day care place now. He really enjoys being with all the other kids."

"Oh, that's great!" Wendy answered. "I'm sure he loves it."

"He does." Luke didn't add that Brayden had also loved Hayley, and both he and his son missed her desperately.

After Wendy had taken their order and walked away, Luke steered their conversation to the ranch. It wasn't long before Wendy returned with their food. When she was gone, Dylan picked up his knife and fork, paused, and then set them down again.

"What?" Luke asked.

"I was just..." His chest rose and fell as he took a deep breath and then let it out. "Do you think I keep to myself too much?"

Luke looked to the counter where Wendy was manning the cash register. "She's married, Dylan."

"What? Who's married?"

"Wendy," Luke answered, nodding in her direction.

Dylan leaned over the table. "Did I say anything about her?" he asked in a loud whisper.

"Well, you said—"

"I asked if you thought I keep to myself too much, not if I should ask somebody for a date."

"Why are you asking me this?"

"Because I know you'll tell me the truth."

Luke's first thought was to quote a line from a well-known movie, but then he realized how serious his brother would take his answer. "I suppose it wouldn't hurt if you got out a little more."

Dylan leaned back, nodding. "I figured you'd say that. It's pretty much the same thing Erin said. Any ideas on how I should go about doing that?"

Luke stared at him. "Not a one."

Nodding again, Dylan picked up his knife and fork. "This sure looks good."

Understanding that the brotherly talk was now over, Luke answered with, "It always is."

He felt better when the conversation returned to the ranch, and by the time they finished their lunch, they'd agreed on ways to handle several things coming up in the future. "Thanks for making me come along today," he told Dylan as they walked to the cash register.

"No problem. You're paying, right?"

For a second, Luke didn't speak, and then he laughed as he stepped up to pay the bill. "You bet."

Darla took the money he handed her with her usual friendly smile. "Where's Brayden today?"

From behind him, he heard the answer. "He's at our place."

Luke turned to acknowledge Dusty, who'd come in the door behind him.

"I wondered if I'd run into you here," Dusty said, and then turned to Darla. "I hope you still have some food left. Morgan's right behind me." He jerked a thumb over his shoulder. "And I think Tanner's on his way, too. The wives gave us the afternoon off. Kate usually has me doing things around the house for her on the weekends. Not today, though. I'm not sure what they're up to, but I have a feeling we'll learn, soon enough."

"They're having their Saturday thing, remember?" Sheriff Morgan Rule said, joining them. "Trish was on the phone giving Hayley directions to our place as I was going out the door. You know how they are about those—"

"Did you say Hayley?" Luke asked.

Morgan turned to look at him. "Yeah. Hayley. The one who was your nanny."

"Brayden's nanny," Luke corrected. He looked at Darla, who had her head down. To Luke, it looked like she was wishing she wasn't around. Surely Hayley wasn't still in town. And if she was, just where the hell was she living? He hadn't thought she knew many people in town, but that probably didn't mean a whole lot in Desperation. She was more than likable and probably made friends easily.

But if she was in town, he wanted to know why no one had told him that she hadn't left. Behind him, he heard Tanner O'Brien greet him and his brother, but he let Dylan answer for both of them, while he stood at the counter, the old cash register separating him from Darla. She had the opportunity to hear most of what went on in town and might have the answers he needed.

"What do you know, Darla?" he asked, keeping his voice low.

She slowly raised her head. "More than you do, obviously, Luke Walker."

"Is she living in town?"

She hesitated, her mouth twisted in a disgusted frown. "I probably shouldn't be telling you this, but you'd find out soon enough, I'm sure. She's living in town, but that's all I'm going to tell you, so don't bother asking me anything else."

He was about to ask if she had the address, but it was pretty clear Hayley didn't want to be found, at least by him.

He took a step back, unable to sort through the feelings that were making him a little crazy. "You're right. I'd find out, sooner or later. But thanks for that much."

Outside in the pickup, he still couldn't think clearly. He was relieved to know Hayley hadn't completely walked out of his life. But she sure hadn't bothered to let him know that she was still around.

"You really miss her, don't you?"

Luke turned to look at his brother, who was driving. "I— You wouldn't believe how much Brayden misses her."

"Don't be stupid, Luke. You two had something special going on, and it wasn't just the employer-employee thing. I don't know what you did to screw it up, but—"

"Me? Why do you think it was me?"

"Just a hunch." The inside of the truck was silent for several seconds. "So what are you going to do about it?"

Luke shook his head. "I don't know. She's just… She's one of a kind."

"Yup. So why don't you do something?"

There was no doubt left in Luke's mind or his heart that somewhere along the way over the past couple of months, he'd fallen in love with Hayley Brooks. He loved her. Brayden loved her. It was as simple as that.

"I don't know what to do," he admitted.

"Well, I may not know much about matters of the heart," Dylan began, speaking slowly and carefully, "but I do know that if I were you, I'd do something pretty damn fast."

"Like what?"

"I can't answer that. Only you can. But I will tell you, little brother, that you're a fool if you don't go after that woman and ask her to marry you."

Luke thought about it for a minute. "Yeah, but I don't know how."

PAIGE PERCHED ON THE EDGE of the small desk in her tiny office just off the waiting room. "You're going to make a fine PA, Hayley. I can't believe you've caught on so fast to everything here, and in such a short time."

Embarrassed, Hayley ducked her head. "Thanks. You're a great doctor to work for. I can't believe I didn't take you up on the offer sooner. Have you heard anything about the new hospital?"

Shaking her head, Paige sighed. "Garrett said the going is slow. I'm not sure if that's good or bad. There's so much red tape involved. I just don't understand why the powers that be can't see how badly it's needed. We could do so much more for so many in a hospital setting." She looked toward the door and moved from the desk. "Cara, have you seen Jenny? I thought she planned to pick up our lunches at the café."

"Oh, dear." The office manager offered an apologetic smile. "Betty called and said there was a package waiting for us at the post office. I just sent Jenny to pick it up." She looked back over her shoulder toward the reception area. "I suppose I could go, but we have patients waiting and—"

"It's all right, Cara. We'll take care of it." Paige turned to look at Hayley. "Would you mind? Normally I wouldn't ask, but we have such a full day."

Hayley smiled. "I don't mind at all. Is it a big order?" she asked Cara.

"Well, there's Dr. Paige, Jenny, you and myself," Cara answered. "Oh, and Fran. Darla usually packs it all in a box for us, but it isn't usually heavy or anything."

"It's not a problem," Hayley assured her. "I'll be back with it as quickly as I can."

"Thanks, Hayley," Paige called to her, as she hurried into the hallway to run the errand.

In the reception area, she slowed. "Trish? Is everything all right?"

Trish raised her blond head from the magazine she was reading and smiled when she saw Hayley. "Just fine. It's time for my, uh, yearly checkup."

"I must have missed seeing your name in the book."

"Oh, Cara squeezed me in. Earlier. When I called," Trish explained.

Hayley sensed something wasn't quite right, but didn't have time to ask more. "I need to run an errand. I'll give you a call later."

Trish nodded. "Yes. Good. Call me later."

Giving her head a little shake and blaming the weirdness on the fact that she'd only had a cinnamon roll for breakfast, Hayley hurried along the sidewalk. Every now and then, she'd see someone passing by in a car, and she'd return the friendly greetings. That's what she liked about Desperation, and she soon reached the café.

As usual, the Chick-A-Lick was doing a brisk business, even though it wasn't Saturday. She didn't stop in very often. Not yet. She knew it wouldn't be long before she'd run into Luke there. When that time came, she hoped to be able to handle it. Just to be certain, while she waited at the register to ask about the order for the clinic, she looked around to make sure he wasn't sitting in one of the booths or at a table. To her relief, she didn't see him.

"Hi, Hayley."

She turned with a smile for Darla. "Is it always this busy during the week?"

Darla's smile was slow and reached her eyes before it hit its widest. "Sometimes. It all depends. Now what can I do for you?"

"Jenny had to run to the post office, so I've come to pick up the order for the doctor's office."

Darla nodded and leaned down, disappearing for a moment. When she straightened, she put a large box on the counter. Opening the flaps, she looked inside, then quickly closed them again. "Here you are. Now the drinks are in the middle. The dinner trays usually keep them pretty stable."

"There should be five orders," Hayley said, as she reached to open the box.

Darla brushed her hands away and placed her own on top of the box. "All there. I saw to them myself." She glanced toward the door. "And just look. There's someone here to help you."

Hayley turned around, just as Luke stepped into the

café. Not sure what to say, she took a step back and then addressed Darla, as if Luke wasn't there. "I—" She cleared her throat and made sure she spoke loud enough for him to hear her. "I can manage on my own."

Picking up the box, which felt entirely too light to contain five dinners and drinks, she squared her shoulders and tried her best to ignore that Luke was blocking her way to the door.

"I'll take that for you," he said, stepping up and relieving her of the box.

"No, I—"

But he was putting the box on the nearest table and paying no attention to her. "Afternoon, Gerald."

The man raised a finger to touch the bill of his gimme cap. "It's shapin' up to be a fine one, I believe."

"I hope so," Luke answered. Turning, he looked directly at Hayley and placed his hands on her shoulders. "We need to talk."

"Not now," she whispered. "I— I need—"

"There are no lunches in the box, Hayley. And if you'll just listen to me, this won't take but a minute."

She knew her mouth was hanging open. "It's *empty*?"

"Afraid so." When she started to move away, he blocked her. "If you look behind me, there are some friends who are going to make sure I get the minutes I'm requesting."

"Requesting?" she asked, her voice rising. "This is how you request?"

"Now calm down. Like I said, it'll only take a minute."

Angry and a little frightened, Hayley turned to Darla for support. But Darla was gone.

"One minute, Hayley. That's all I'm asking."

She refused to look directly at him and pressed her lips together to keep from saying anything…as if she could focus on something to say with his hands moving slowly up and down her arms.

"I just want to tell you how sorry I am," he said, not bothering to keep his voice down. "I never had any intention of taking advantage of you—"

"Luke!" Her gaze met his. "Everyone is watching. And *listening*."

"Don't worry about it."

"But—"

"Hey, Luke, why don't you try kissing her?" Dusty, standing guard at the door, suggested.

"Yeah, it worked for Dusty," someone in the corner of the café shouted.

Hayley couldn't believe what was happening. "Don't you dare, Luke Walker. Not with all these people—"

But she couldn't finish. His lips were on hers in a kiss she couldn't fight, even if she'd wanted to.

"Now you're on the right track," Dusty announced. "What do you think, folks?"

"Got a rope on ya, Dusty?" Gerald asked. "You know, just in case."

"Nah, it'd take too long to get it out of my pickup, and I don't want to miss anything."

Slowly, Luke ended the kiss, but he didn't let go of her. Hayley stared at the crowd around them, and then looked at Luke to see him grinning down at her.

"I think I can get it done without a rope," he said, "but thanks for the offer."

Hayley saw movement behind Dusty, and Kate

stepped out. "Just give in and agree to whatever he says, Hayley. Once they have their minds made up, Desperation men don't give up."

From farther away, she heard Trish add, "I'll give that a solid second." Friendly laughter filled the café.

"Luke—"

"Yeah, I know. I've probably done enough harm, but…" He looked around at the crowd and announced, "I think we need to take this private."

There was a loud, collective groan, along with some grumbling. He ignored it as he slipped an arm around her and steered her past the long counter to a tiny hallway, where he knocked on a closed door. "Could we borrow your office?"

The door opened to reveal a grinning Darla. "I wondered how long it was going to take you," she said, looking from one to the other. Then she scooted past them into the hall. "It's all yours. Just don't steam up the windows." Stopping, she looked over her shoulder, her eyes narrowed and calculating. "Shoot. There aren't any windows."

With a wink, Darla was gone, and Luke held the door open, while Hayley stepped into the cell-size office. "Not much room," he said, looking around.

Hayley, who'd moved into the small space where two metal chairs faced a battered metal desk, couldn't argue. There was barely enough room to stand. Behind the desk, a threadbare swivel chair took up nearly every inch of space, along with an old file cabinet that, by the look of it, must have been used during the Civil War.

"Now where was I?" Luke asked. "Oh, yeah. I remember." His hands slipped around her waist, and he pulled her closer. "I think this is the spot."

When the rush of heat swept through her, Hayley tried to pull away. "What do you want, Luke?" she asked, wishing her voice hadn't wobbled.

He leaned back, and she felt his gaze move over her face. "That's an honest question," he said, "and I'll give you an equally honest answer. I want you."

Hayley's heart skipped a beat, and she wished it hadn't. She couldn't deal with this if she couldn't keep her emotions under control. "I'm not up for grabs."

His smile vanished, replaced by a deep frown. "That's not what I mean."

She shook her head. If she could turn back the clock— But she couldn't. "I never should have insisted on being a live-in."

"It was the only way to make it work. Even I recognized that. None of this is your fault. I lost control the other night, but it wasn't a spur-of-the-moment thing. I've been wanting to do it since I first saw you coming up the walk to the house, so it wouldn't have mattered if you'd been a live-in or not."

Her throat clogged with tears, but a nervous giggle managed to escape. "You looked so funny with Brayden wrapped around your legs," she said, laughing around the tears that threatened to spill. "I was so nervous."

He pulled her closer. "What would have happened to Brayden when he was sick, if you hadn't come back after your class?"

She couldn't look at him. "You would have managed."

"Would I? I didn't even have a thermometer that worked. Hayley, please, please come back."

Steeling herself against the emotions that threatened to give her away, she shook her head. "I can't."

He tipped her face up with a finger under her chin. "Of course you can. Brayden and I need you in our lives."

"No. I'm working at the doctor's office now, and I'm not going to leave there."

"You don't—"

She shook her head again, cutting him off. Unable to answer, she closed her eyes. If they'd been honest... If she hadn't insisted on being a live-in... If she hadn't had too much to drink... She'd botched it all, thinking her attraction to him would go away if she ignored it. Instead, she'd fallen in love with him, and all he wanted was a nanny for his son.

"Look at me, Hayley."

Reluctant to do what he asked, she warred with herself, certain she was headed for more heartbreak. But she gave in and slowly opened her eyes. She knew in an instant that she'd misjudged him. She'd been wrong, and she could see it in his eyes.

"I love you, Hayley," he said, his voice quiet, yet strong and confident. "I want us to be a real family. You, me and Brayden."

Stunned, she could barely speak. "Are you..."

"Proposing?" His smile grew bigger. "You bet I am. And as soon as you say you'll marry me, we can get out of here."

Pure joy filled her as she looked up at him. But nothing was settled. Not yet. "There are a few things you need to know."

His eyebrows went up, but he nodded. "Okay."

"I'm going to continue working as a nurse at the doctor's office—"

"I like that."

She smiled, then frowned. "I'm not done. Nothing—and I mean nothing—is going to get in the way of finishing my degree this summer."

"We'll be right there, Brayden and I, when they hand you that diploma."

"Paige has already asked if I'll join her as a PA. I've accepted."

"Wow. We'll have an almost-a-doctor in the family," he teased, but immediately sobered. "I couldn't be prouder, Hayley."

"And one more thing," she continued, secretly treasuring his words. "I'm going to live in my apartment, until we're married."

He closed his eyes and groaned. "I was afraid of that."

But one look at him, and she knew it didn't matter to him, only she did. "Then it's all good?

Opening his eyes, he smiled. "It's all good."

And then he kissed her, long, deep and filled with the promise of a beautiful life together. She'd never felt so loved.

A knock on the door broke through the cloud of passion surrounding her, and she heard a male voice.

"Hey, you two. Folks out here are wondering if you have something you want to share. You know, like are you going to get married or something? They're about ready to storm the office there, where you're hiding out, and to tell the truth, I can't take on the whole town."

She not only heard, but felt Luke's rumble of laughter. "Be right there," he called to Dusty. To Hayley, he said, "You're sure you want to spend the rest of your life in a town that knows everything you do and say?"

She laughed and pressed her hand to his cheek. "You must have forgotten that I grew up in a town even smaller than this. More gossip per person."

"Good point," he said and laughed, too. "So you're ready to face them?"

"They're our friends, so, yes, I'm ready."

"Then let's get this done, or we'll have to stay here and have our meals ordered in."

He stopped her laughter with a kiss that made her forget everything except him. When he slowly pulled away and released her, he moved to the door. "You're sure?"

"I'm sure. Of everything, especially you."

Out in the hallway, he scooped her up and into his arms, carrying her back the way they'd come. "Smile," he whispered. "It'll make people wonder what we've been up to."

She couldn't stop laughing and had to press her lips together. Ahead, she saw that the café was full of people, all with eyes on the two of them.

"Anybody wanna take a guess as to what they decided?" Gerald asked in a room where the drop of a pin could have been heard.

Luke caught her gaze as he continued to walk toward the door, a question in his eyes. She shook her head. *Let them guess.*

As they passed Sheriff Rule, he pointed to the star pinned to his shirt. "It's my duty to warn you, Luke, kidnapping is a felony in this state."

Luke nodded. "I'll keep that in mind, Morgan."

Someone—Hayley didn't see who—had the good grace to open the door when they reached it. "Thank you," she called back to the crowd in the café, as Luke carried her out the door and on to his pickup.

When she was settled next to him in the truck, and after a kiss that curled her toes, she asked, "Where are we going?"

"Home," he said, turning to look at her. "Home to our little boy."

* * * *

Be sure to look for Dylan Walker's story,
Designs on the Cowboy,
available in June 2013!

The CALLAHAN COWBOY *series continues with Tina Leonard's HIS CALLAHAN BRIDE'S BABY.*

Falcon has his work cut out for him trying to convince Taylor to be his wife—but if his proposal doesn't work, he'll lose his ranch land to his siblings!

Taylor Waters was one of Diablo's "best" girls. She had a reputation for being wild at heart. Untamable. Men threw themselves at her feet and she walked all over them with a sweet-natured smile.

Falcon Chacon Callahan studied the well-built brunette behind the counter of Banger's Bait and Tackle diner. He'd talked the owner, Jillian, into selling him one last beer, even though the diner usually closed at the stroke of midnight on the weekends. It was his Saturday night off from Rancho Diablo, and he hadn't wanted to do anything but relax and consider what he was going to do with his life once his job at the ranch was over.

Taylor was more of an immediate interest. She smiled that cute pixie smile at him and Falcon sipped his beer, deciding on a whim—some might call it a hunch—to toss his heart into the Taylor tizzy. "I need a wife," he said.

"So I hear. So we all hear." She came and sat on the bar stool next to him. "You'll get it figured out eventually, Falcon."

"Marry me, Taylor."

"I know you're not drunk enough to propose, Falcon. You're just crazy, like we've always heard." She smiled so adorably, all of the sting fled her words. In fact, she was so cute about her opinion that Falcon felt his chest expand.

"I leave crazy to my brothers. My sister is the wild and crazy one. Me, I'm somewhere on the other side of the

HAREXP0413

spectrum." He leaned over and kissed her lightly on the lips. Falcon grinned. "What's your answer, cupcake?"

"You're not serious." Taylor shook her head. "I've known you for over a year. Of all the Callahans, you're the one the town's got odds on being last to the altar." She got up and sashayed to the register. His eyes followed her movements hungrily. "A girl would be a fool to fall for you, Falcon Callahan."

That did not sound like a *yes.*

But Falcon is a cowboy who always gets his way!
Watch for his story coming in April 2013, only from
Harlequin® American Romance®.

HAREXP0413

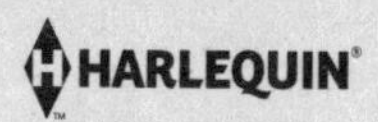

Another touching tale from

MARIN THOMAS

No Ordinary Cowboy

After the death of his best friend, border patrol agent Tony Bravo needs a job transfer to San Diego to help him move on and forget. Lucy Durango is making him rethink his plans. With Tony's help, Lucy is determined to make amends for her role in her brother's death and hopes her efforts are enough to convince Tony to forgive her. But she doesn't expect to learn that Tony feels just as much guilt as she does, making her believe that together they can find the peace they've both been searching for and a future together.

Available from Harlequin® American Romance®
April 2, 2013!

www.Harlequin.com

HAR75451